Reluctant Bloom

Arabell Spencer

Chapter 1

"Watch out!" I squeezed my eyes shut after the near miss.
"Jessa, please. You need to pay attention. You almost hit that
guy!"

Jessa rolled her eyes at me and dramatically fixated
on the road ahead. "You know, Lanie, nagging is your worst
habit. Well, one of them. It's so boring."

"I'm sorry. Just – that guy on the bike, he was just so
close to my side. It's … Whatever. Sorry."

"Okay, so back to the topic at hand." Jessa cleared her
throat. "I have no patience for Steve anymore. My mom is all
for it. Dad, too, for that matter, but, God, he's so boring."

Jessa had two favorite words – boring and lame. It
kind of made up her world view. She continued talking about
Steve's lack of almost anything redeeming while I murmured
my agreement and nodded. Really, I thought Steve was a
pretty nice guy. He was attractive, and he really liked Jessa.
He was solid. I think that's what Jessa meant when she called
him boring. Or maybe not. I certainly got the boring label
from her often enough, and I don't think anyone would have

described me as solid. But Steve was solid … and Jessa was Jessa. It wasn't entirely her fault she was easily bored.

"You know, making out with him is like making out with Ethan. It's so lame." She crossed her eyes and stuck out her tongue.

"Gross! Ethan is your brother, Jess. What is wrong with you?"

"Exactly. It's like making out with my brother. He's got nothing going on at all. After he takes me to this concert next week, I'm out."

Thinking about the concert she was looking forward to, Jessa forgot the road again while she scrolled through Spotify on her phone for a new track. I tried to hide my discomfort, but she saw me tense.

"Seriously, Lanie. Stop. I'm fine. I can see everything on this wide-open road. Life is good. And get that sad puppy look off your face. Stop thinking about Ethan and making out and whatever I said. I'm sorry I brought him up. Just move on."

"I'm good, I'm good. It's forgotten." I looked at the trees whizzing by as we made our way out of town. It was a rare Saturday that I had off work, so Jessa and I were headed to the beach. It was really too cold. We knew all we would be able to do was walk a bit and look at the water, but the long

Maine winter was finally starting to thaw. The sun was shining, so who cared that it was only fifty degrees?

Ready to shift into more pleasant conversation, I said, "So you know Zeke?" as I gave Jessa a side-eye glance. She loved my work gossip. She said it was much better than thinking about her boring days at the bank.

"Yeah. What happened? Did he finally actually screw someone in the bathroom?"

"What? No! At least I hope not. No, he was working the register while I was out back for a minute. When I came to the front, I heard some Beecham kids talking crap about his piercings and hair. Saying things like 'freak' and 'burnout' and stuff. They weren't loud, but he had literally just taken their order and you could totally hear them."

"Oh my God, what did Mr. Pierced-in-all-the-right-places do?"

"Spit," I said, conflicted about the memory but knowing it would entertain Jessa.

"What, like on them? Seriously? That's lame."

"No," I said, starting to laugh as I remembered the rich Beecham College kids drinking their coffee. "No, in the coffee," I managed to finish between giggles.

Jessa was starting to smile a bit, so I continued. "He took a paper cup and went to the back before he started their drinks. I went to see if he needed my help, but he told me to piss off."

"You're his supervisor, Lanie!"

"In name only. You know Glenn doesn't actually have me make any decisions or lead anything. Anyway, Zeke had this cup of spit, and he was pouring it in each one. I mean, it was really mean and disgusting, but they were so awful to say those things about him. I know I should have tried to stop him, but I also know there was zero chance he would listen to me."

"Spit, huh?" Jessa asked. "Funny, but still lame. And clichéd. I thought he was a little more badass. I mean, would a coffee house brawl be too much trouble?"

Jessa and I laughed as we imagined all the things she wished Zeke would have done to make her life more interesting.

The beach we had chosen for this adventure was one that had a little sand and a little rock – my favorite when there was some of each. After hiking for a half hour or so, we had collected what we needed and looked around to determine where we would build our fairy house. We'd been doing this since we were kids. The little houses could get pretty elaborate. Baby pinecone people with seaweed hair, tiny shells in a circle for a fire ring, rocks and reeds and pine boughs tucked into a driftwood shelter. All this would be lovingly and painstakingly created and then preserved in pictures on my phone. I wanted to start an Instagram account to share our creations, but Jessa said it was lame. Lame or not, it was something we did together that she still enjoyed. I wasn't going to push it.

"Lanie," Jessa said in her sing-song voice that prepared me for something I knew I wasn't going to like.

"Yeah?" I asked cautiously.

She screwed up her face into a pout. "Stop it! You're already defensive. Seriously. I have something to talk to you about."

"Okay. Sorry," I said. It wasn't defensiveness I was feeling; it was fear. I never knew what Jessa was going to want. "Go ahead. I'm not being defensive. What is it?"

"It's just – you know that guy Jet? That I met last week when I took you on that pub crawl?"

"Sure. Yeah, the guy you ditched me for halfway through the night? That guy?" Maybe I was feeling defensive. "I told you I didn't even want to go that night."

"It's not ditching. Obviously, if one of us meets a guy, the other one is supportive. I mean, you know that. Stop it – you are being defensive, Lanie!"

"No, I'm good. I'm fine," I said, telling myself to be fair. "What about him?"

"Welllll …" Jessa dragged out. "He kind of needs a place to stay, and I told him he could crash with us."

I closed my eyes and took in a deep breath. I took a couple more, knowing there was no point in arguing. If Jessa had already told him he could move in, it was a done deal. It was Jessa's name on the lease even if I did pay half the rent (more, usually) and for most of the groceries. And even if it had been my name on the lease, I still knew this would have been headed the same direction.

"Yeah?" I finally asked, meeting her eyes. She had that look she got when she knew she was going to get her way.

"Yeah. It'll be cool. He works at the bar, so you'll practically never see him. He'll get in really late after you're asleep. He said he could crash on the couch – or maybe with me. We'll see."

"And Steve?"

"I told you! The concert is next week. Then Steve is done. He doesn't need to know this is happening. And he doesn't need to know what already happened," Jessa giggled as she waggled her eyebrows.

"Yeah, okay. Just – Jessa, are you sure?" I asked, fully aware there was no changing her mind. "That guy seemed pretty sketchy."

"Totally sure. He's super hot, and I like him! And he just needs a place to crash for a bit. No big deal."

"Got it. Yeah." I fiddled with a few small stones we had fashioned into a fairy fire ring. "So, when is this happening?"

"Tonight!" she practically squealed. "We're going to meet up with him after this! Just, seriously, make sure you don't say anything to Steve. Or my parents! And don't be like you always are when other people are around. I mean, we're going to live with him. Just talk and be yourself. I mean, don't be your weird self. Be your normal self. Your Jessa self. That's the one I like."

"Stop being such a bitch!" I said as I shoved Jessa over into the sand from her crouch in front of the fairy house.

"You know you love me – bitch and all," she said as she dramatically splayed herself out on the beach.

"I do," I said, laughing and holding out my hand to help her up.

I wasn't an idiot. I did know Jessa was a bitch. But she was my bitch. When I really needed it, she had my back. Every time. And she was really all I had in that department.

And I got her. I did. She was self-centered and selfish and a little lazy – but she was loving and sweet, too. I was terrified of pretty much everything, and she was fearless. We balanced each other. She was like her mom, except Jessa actually liked me. Thank God for that. Ethan was like their dad. Jessa didn't get that gene. And thank God for that as well.

After hiking and finishing our fairy house, we sat in front of the waves, eating some lemon poppy seed muffins I had made that morning and warming ourselves with coffee from the big thermos I had packed. We laughed at the shivering tourists who didn't know to wear hats and heavy sweaters to visit the Maine beach in early May, and, finally, we shook the sand off and settled back into Jessa's car. Indicative of her mellow mood after our sunshine and fresh air, and after she had achieved my acquiescence on the whole Jet thing, she put some chill music on, and we slowly began heading down the road leading out of the state park.

"Jessa, I am not kidding this time. You have to stop!" Just as I squealed "stop", Jessa's little car rear-ended the truck in front of us. She had been paying attention to her phone, which was buzzing with an incoming text.

"Lanie, are you okay?" Jessa cried and looked over. She started frantically patting me all over. "Are you okay? Are you sure? Are you okay?"

"I'm fine. I'm good. Are you okay?"

"Well, yeah." She paused a beat, breathing a little too quickly. Then she blinked hard and said, "I mean, I was only going like ten miles per hour. It's no big deal. Whatever. Shit. My dad is going to kill me. But, really, whatever. It's fine, right?"

"I mean, we're fine. Yeah. I'm not sure about your car. And I'm really not sure about that angry-looking man headed our way."

"Shit. This can't happen again. My parents made me get off their insurance and I kind of let mine lapse a little bit and—"

"Jessa! Are you serious?"

"It's fine. It's totally fine." She smoothed out her hair and licked her lips. She took three deep breaths. "Watch and learn."

I did watch as Jessa hopped out of the car and flashed her self-described "sexy smile". The man looked incredulous as he approached her. He started shouting and gesturing back to his truck. Really, there wasn't too much damage. We had been going slowly since we had barely left the parking lot when it happened. She hadn't seen that a trail of cars had stopped to let some animal cross the road. A squirrel or something – I hadn't been able to see. I hadn't warned her because we were creeping along, and I had assumed she'd seen the obvious line of cars. I had wanted to warn her just in case, but I was also trying to avoid irritating her again.

While the man got closer to Jessa on the other side of the car, I stepped out and took a look. Jessa's headlight was shattered and there was a small dent on the part of her hood where her car had hit the bottom of the truck's bumper. There didn't look to be any damage to the truck itself, but the truck bumper was barely hanging on to one side. When the man gestured to the truck, it didn't look like he was gesturing at the damage. I looked past that where it seemed his arm was indicating. From the back window of the truck, I saw a little face and a tiny pair of hands pressed to the glass. The little boy stared out at the scene, looking terrified. I didn't blame him. The man was scary.

As much as I hated talking to pretty much anyone other than Jessa, I could tell her charms were not effective this time. As I re-focused on their interaction and approached their side a little, I could hear Jessa pleading, "No, please don't call the police. Please! It's not so much damage. I'm good for it. No need for insurance. I can cover it. Let me give you my number, and you can tell me when you have a repair estimate. I'll cover it. I promise."

"Are you fucking kidding me? You're good for it? No need for insurance? Are you actually drunk right now?"

"No! I—"

"Hi. Um, hello," I interrupted, forcing myself to speak up. The man shifted his eyes to me and waited. "Hi. Um. I'm Lanie." I willed my voice to stop shaking. "Lanie Billings. Sorry about all of this. Um, is your son okay? Are you okay?"

He gave a hard look to Jessa, implying maybe that should have been a concern she had expressed by now. "Yeah," he reluctantly replied. "At least I think so. No thanks to your friend here. I can't believe this!" He turned quickly and started heading back to his truck door, pulling his phone out as he walked.

"Um, hey, um, sir …" I had no idea how to address him. He wasn't *that* much older than I was, but I was desperate to try anything to get him to give Jessa a break. "Yeah, just wait please?" I wrung my hands together. "Can we figure this out? I mean, the important thing is no one got hurt. There's not much damage," I said, carefully touching the truck bumper to make sure it wasn't actually about to fall off.

"What, so you two got drunk at the beach and thought it was fine to just drive away?" He directed his question menacingly at Jessa.

"No! No, of course not," I said. "We weren't drinking at all. I mean, we drank coffee, but not like you mean. This is all just an accident. Surely you've made a mistake before." He gave me a hard stare before I continued. "Can we just figure out a solution here? Is there anything we can do?" I looked him over closely as he stood frozen with his phone in his hand by his truck door. The cars that had been behind us kept creeping around our little scene at a crawl.

"Um, look," I said, grasping at straws. "I could give you my ID or something. You could, um, you could hold on to it until Jessa pays you for the repairs. Then you would know we weren't going to disappear, right? Please?"

"Yeah!" Jessa piped up. "Yeah! Lanie can give you her ID. That would work. Go get it, Lanie. This will work. Hurry up!"

"Daddy," the little boy called from the driver's side window. "Daddy, can we go home now? I want to see Milo!" The man rubbed both hands over his face – hard. After blowing out a sigh, he looked at Jessa and then back to his son.

He walked slowly, but deliberately, back to Jessa. He stood right in front of her and looked down at her from his six-foot-two height. His deep, measured breathing and towering stature made him seem like a fire-breathing dragon in front of her. The anger was still at DEFCON 1, but he clearly was also distracted by his son, who was ready to get out of there. "Right. Here's what we're going to do." He pulled his wallet from his back pocket and fished out a business card. "Give me your driver's license," he said to Jessa.

"No," Jessa protested. "Lanie. Lanie is going to give you hers. I need mine."

"Again," the dragon said somewhat patiently, certainly more calmly than the fury in his eyes suggested. "Here's what's going to happen. You're giving me your license." He pointed straight at Jessa. "I have no use for your little friend's ID. You. You are giving me your license. I am giving you this card for my farm."

"Your farm? Why do I need that?" Jessa asked. "Just have your mechanic call me or whatever."

"Stop. Talking." He lifted his hands, palms up, toward Jessa. "Please, just stop talking."

"Daddy!" the boy called again. "Please, let's go!"

"You will come to my farm starting on Monday morning, and you will work on my farm for five days next week. You will work *hard* for five days. Then I'll give you back your license. If you want this back and don't want me to report this to the police or the insurance company, this is what's happening. And if you don't show up Monday morning, I'll know you've changed your mind about me reporting this incident. That's it. You put everyone at risk driving like that without paying attention. You could have hurt my son. Or your friend." He spared me the tiniest glance. "Or yourself." He stalked around Jessa and opened her door. "Get your license. You have five seconds, or I'm going to plan B."

"You're insane," Jessa grumbled. But she did make a move for her purse in the car. It was clear the dragon was serious. The way he was glaring at her was intense, but I could also see he was shaken up. I could imagine how scary it must have been to be hit like that with a child in the car. He glanced at me again, then back at his son, who was now crying a little.

I watched the little boy, feeling terrible for him and afraid the dragon was going to change his mind.

Jessa backed out of the car and childishly thrust her license toward him. He took it and said, "Jessaline Michaud."

He looked over at me and asked, "Is that right? Is she Jessaline?"

"Of course it's right," Jessa snapped. "Why are you asking her?"

"Just checking." He shifted his gaze to me very briefly again.

"It's right. Jessa … Jessaline."

"Monday morning," he said, looking intensely at Jessa. "Eight sharp. Or I make a quick call." He checked his bumper briefly to make sure it was going to hold and then moved to get into his truck.

"Asshole," Jessa said, not quite under her breath.

"Jessa, shut up," I breathed out as we both got in the car. I watched the truck pull away and looked over to Jessa, who seemed angrier than she deserved to feel.

Chapter 2

I lay in my bed, wondering if it was safe to venture out into the living room. Jet had presumably come to crash after his shift at the bar the night before. We had met up with him after the beach incident. Jessa had gone on and on about how horrible the man in the truck had been – Max Parker. That's what his card had said. Parker Farm in Stoneton, about twenty minutes away from where Jessa and I lived. Not surprisingly, Jessa somehow made it Max's fault. She complained that he should have put his hazard lights on. I pointed out there was a long line of stopped traffic in front of him, and it hadn't come up as a surprise. She complained that he was an uptight rule-follower to want to call the police and insurance company. I pointed out that he seemed primarily concerned about the danger his son had been in. It went on and on. Jet grunted and appeased Jessa, stroking her in all the places he could while sitting in a public Starbucks. Jessa had given him a key, and they'd agreed he would let himself in after he finished working later that night.

Was he out there on the couch right now? Or had he gone into Jessa's room? One way or another, I was going to have to go out there. I needed to get ready for my shift at the coffee shop. Technically, I was the manager of the shop – a result of holding down a barista job in the same place for so long. I'd started there when I was in high school and, at twenty-four, I was still there. The manager title didn't amount to much. It gave me about a dollar more per hour and very little else. The owner was very invested in the day-to-day business and didn't appreciate change or suggestions for improvement.

Sighing, I got out of bed, pulled an oversized sweatshirt over the tank top I had slept in, and grabbed some soft leggings. I pulled my hair up into a bun, figuring that was the best I could do before actually getting some time in the bathroom. If I ran into Jet before then, so be it. I crept out to the living room and, not seeing anyone walking around, streaked into the bathroom without stopping to look at the couch. When I made my way out a bit later, I ran right into Jessa, who had clearly been waiting for me just outside the door.

"Shh!" she prompted with a finger to her pursed lips. I tried to rein in my gasp and gave her bug eyes. "Jet's still sleeping," she said, averting her eyes to her bedroom. Well, that answered one question.

I made my way to the kitchen and started the coffee. "What are you doing up?" I asked her as I took my favorite mug out of the cabinet. "It's Sunday. You don't have to work."

"I need to talk to you," she said, grabbing the mug out of my hands for herself. I turned around and took my second favorite. "Okay," she started, "I need your help."

"Jessa, I'm fine with Jet being here, but I want nothing more to do with him ... With this ..." I gestured as if Jet's offensive frame were in front of me. "I don't know what you want me to do for him, but I don't want to be around him any more than I have to be."

"No, no – not Jet. Jet's fine. He doesn't need anything – not from you. Ha! If you know what I mean. No, it's about this farm thing."

"Jess, you have to do this." I dropped an English muffin in the toaster. "You have no choice here. I can't even imagine the fine you would have to pay or whatever happens if you have a crash and don't have car insurance. You need to get the time off from work. Do whatever it takes."

Trying to talk Jessa into making smarter decisions was familiar ground, and I tried, as I usually did, to help her make the better decision both for herself but also out of some self-interest. Her problems were always our problems.

"I actually think this is a good solution since you probably would have a hard time paying for the repairs. I looked up the cost of a bumper for that truck and it's more than you make in a week."

"There's no way I can get that many days off. Like, I can call in sick for a few days, but that's as good as it gets. *But*, I have a great idea. And it will actually be fun!" She clapped her hands and beamed at me.

My heart sank. "Why do I think this doesn't sound like something that's going to be fun?"

"So, five days of work for one person would only be two and a half days of work if there are two of us doing it! And we could hang out together and, you know, live the farm life for a few days. Pet some horses, look cute in jeans and boots. Fun, right? I know you can get someone to cover for a few days. It will be great for both of us! So fun, right?"

"Um, no," I said, adding butter to my breakfast. "Not fun. And I don't think what you're describing is an accurate depiction of farm life. And I can't get the time off. *And* Max Parker doesn't seem like the kind of guy who would go for your solution to this problem. He was pretty clear it was his way, or he'd call the police."

"Lanie ..." Jessa gave me a pathetically sad look. Her eyes had dropped to the kitchen bar where she sat, and when she looked up at me, her eyes were shimmering with unshed tears. "I can't do it his way. I really need your help. I need you to go with me and help me convince him that he will get the same work done if it's both of us for two days. Or two and a half, if he really insists. You know they already hate me at the bank. No one will cover for me, and I can't go the whole week without a paycheck. Seriously, I just need your help." The tears were coming freely now. Even though I knew she was skilled at emotional manipulation, I loved her too much to be okay seeing her in distress.

"Fine. Fine, Jessa. Stop crying." I reached out to her to hug her. "I'll see what I can do. I really don't know if I can get someone to cover on such short notice, but I'll try. I'll really try. I promise."

Jessa hugged me tightly and lifted her face up to me from where she sat on one of the bar stools. "I knew you wouldn't let me down. Thank you. Really, Lanie. Thank you." She jumped up and kissed me all over my face. She grabbed both our cups, filled them with coffee, and carefully gave me the one she knew was my favorite. "I love you, Lanie. I knew you would help me fix this."

***

Very early the next morning, I cringed as I crept into Jessa's bedroom and shook her awake while trying to avoid even looking at the creepy Jet sleeping next to her. "Jessa," I hissed, "wake up. We have to get to the farm. Eight o'clock sharp, remember? We can't be late."

"Five more minutes," she mumbled.

Luckily, I was experienced in Jessa's early morning habits and had planned for this. It took two more times of shaking her and giving her "five more minutes" before she actually rolled out of bed. When she emerged to join me for breakfast, I marched her right back to her room and told her she had to change her clothes. She had put together an outfit of a slinky tank top with a sexy long cardigan, tight skinny jeans and heeled brown booties. If she had more time to shop, I was sure the outfit would have been complete with cowboy boots and hat. She had done her best with what she had.

"I don't know what you're picturing, Jessa, but what you need to picture is that farm we went to on Maple Syrup Sunday when we were sixteen. Remember that? That's what you need to dress for." In Maine, the maple syrup producers would open their farms in the spring to the public and we'd gone one year. It was really fun seeing the "sugar shacks" where they turned the sap into syrup, and they had things like maple candy and servings of ice cream topped with maple syrup. It smelled amazing and was a good time, but it was during mud season in Maine on farms with hundreds of people tromping around. It was muddy, cold, and, depending on the farm (and apart from right inside the sugar shack), really smelly.

"Old jeans, old sweatshirt, sturdy shoes. Go!" I said, shoving her back into her bedroom.

Just before eight, I drove my little Toyota into Parker Farm. I sighed as I thought about how all of this would have been avoided had I just driven to the beach that day. Hindsight and all that.

Jessa had complied with the wardrobe. Well, not the suggestion that she wear old things, but she had at least toned it down to simpler, warmer items. I had dressed in a plain light purple sweatshirt, jeans, and hiking books. I also had a pair of slim wool gloves with me and had pulled a beige wool beanie over my hair. My hair was that kind of blonde that barely had any pigment – not the kind of trendy blonde streaks that were woven through Jessa's hair. She was always telling me I should get lowlights, explaining that I was all one color with my pale skin and pale hair and that I just kind of disappeared. She wasn't wrong. Even my eyes were a light hazel that didn't stand out much. But she also couldn't understand why blending in was more of a goal of mine than standing out was.

"This place doesn't look like a farm," Jessa announced as I put the car in park.

"Care to elaborate?" I asked. "I see fields and giant greenhouses. That seems farm-like to me."

"Where's the red barn? Where are the horses and stables and—"

"His card said Parker Farm, not Parker Ranch."

"Right," Jessa said, checking her makeup in the visor mirror. "Well, this is definitely going to be boring."

"Just boring?" I looked over at her and added with a smirk, "Lame, too, maybe?"

"Yes," she laughed as I had hoped she would. "Totally boring and totally lame."

As Max Parker approached my car, Jessa and I stepped out of it. No matter how much Jessa blamed Max for everything, he was still an incredibly attractive man, and she couldn't completely hide her excitement about the opportunity to flirt with him again. He was tall with dark hair. Totally fit, which made sense given his work. And, despite his angry, uptight demeanor when we'd met him, his clothes, truck, and his home gave off a laid-back feeling. Unlike Jessa, my reaction to attractive men was to become even more shy and awkward. So, while she hopped out of the car, I shuffled out, keeping my head down, afraid to see his reaction to my being there.

"Had your chauffeur bring you, I see," he said to Jessa, ignoring me.

"Well, sort of. I actually wanted to talk to you about that."

"About what?" Max scowled at Jessa. "It's your problem you need a ride – I'm not providing transportation for your punishment if that's what you're getting at."

"No, not at all. Lanie is perfectly willing to bring us back and forth. It's just—"

"Us? Bring *us* back and forth?"

"Well, yeah," Jessa said. "That's what I wanted to talk to you about. Lanie is a really hard worker and, together, we can do the same work to pay off the repairs to your truck in half the time. Perfect, right? You get your work done sooner and then we get out of your way. See? Win-win!" She kept trying out her arsenal of seductive looks and poses. Max was unaffected.

"No," Max said unequivocally.

"No? What no? Why no? This is perfect!" Jessa was working hard to sell her idea. "I can't take a week off from work, and this way I can still pay you back with a week's worth of work. It's ideal for both of us."

"And your friend?" he continued to avoid talking to me, directing his question to Jessa even though I was standing right there. "Is this ideal for her too?"

"Pshh, Lanie? She doesn't mind. She wants to help me. That's what friends do."

"No. Not interested in this solution. Your little friend can head on home and pick you up later when you're finished. You have five days here. Get used to it."

"You are really insane, you know that? Is this a power trip for you?" Jessa downshifted her anger as a thought clearly occurred to her. "Or maybe you just want me around longer?" Jessa tried again with the smile and sidled up to him.

"Fuck no. Back off, lady. You need to learn some responsibility. You need to learn a lot actually. The five days isn't to make up for my truck. It's to make sure you pay for what you did – to learn there are consequences for that kind of stupid shit. Not paying attention, being reckless, driving without insurance!" Clearly, he had figured out Jessa's reluctance to trade information. "You know, it could have ended differently. Someone could have been hurt …" he trailed off. "Five days. Get used to it. Or you know what?

This was a stupid idea. I'm just going to make a phone call and wash my hands of this."

"But I can't!" Jessa whimpered a little. She was close to turning on the waterworks – whether for effect or for real, who knew. Either way, it wasn't going to work with Max. That much was clear.

"Um, Mr. Parker, sir, could I just …" I tried to speak loudly enough for him to hear me. I couldn't count the number of times I had gotten up the nerve to speak to someone only to be completely ignored, finally realizing they literally hadn't heard me.

"Max," he said. "Not Mr. Parker. Not sir. It's Max." He gave me a quick glance and turned his attention back to Jessa.

"Okay, um, Max. So, please, could you reconsider? I really understand what you're saying, but Jessa isn't kidding about her work. It is hard to get five days in a row off. And I was already able to work it out at my job. I'm happy to help. I mean, hey, um, I was in the car too, so I should really put in my time anyway. I should have stopped it from happening."

"Do you hear this?" Max said to Jessa. "Do you hear what your friend is saying? She's trying to take responsibility – something you still haven't done!" He turned around and walked a few steps before backtracking to us again, taking in a long-suffering breath. "Fine," he finally said. "You win. Take advantage of your friend. Not my problem. That's between the two of you."

"She's not taking advantage—" I started to say.

"Meet me over by that high tunnel in five minutes," Max interrupted, pointing to a massive structure about fifty yards behind his New England-style farmhouse. In typical fashion, the house did actually have an attached barn – just not the type Jessa had expected in her vision of a ranch movie set.

"High tunnel?" Jessa asked.

"Greenhouse," Max said and walked away, muttering to himself as he went. "Stupid idea, fucking stupid idea."

***

"Don't you have a tractor or even one of those spinny things you push?" Jessa asked incredulously.

"Sure, I do." Max was focused on Jessa, allowing me a minute to fully take him in. He had on jeans and a dark green Henley with the sleeves pushed up to his elbows. Now that his eyes weren't flashing with the anger that had been there in our first meeting, I could see they were a rich brown without any other flecks of color. He glanced at me for a second, and I quickly averted my eyes. "But I also have extra labor I don't normally have and using the broadfork produces great soil. Your job is to turn the soil in this high tunnel."

"Um, how big is this?" I asked quietly.

"Thirty by ninety." He directed his attention firmly to Jessa. "Take the broadfork and lift the soil, then use this claw to knock out the clumps, and then you'll use the rake to smooth things out. I'll show you a few times. I suggest you pay close attention because there's a right way and several wrong ways. The soil will show if you're not doing it right, and you'll have to do it again." He raised his eyebrows and waited for Jessa to acknowledge she understood.

"Right," Jessa said. "Okay, let's see it then."

Panicked that we would never get it right, I pulled out my phone and clicked on the camera app, so I could video the demonstration. I filmed as Max lifted the soil with the broadfork, creating a row of the raised soil he worked. He went to switch the broadfork with the claw tool once he had a half row lifted, and glanced up at me while he made the switch. "What is she doing?" he asked Jessa. "This isn't for some YouTube channel or Instagram page or whatever shit you plan to do with that. Tell her to cut it out."

Mortified, I slipped my camera in my back pocket. "I was just trying to save it, so I could make sure to do it right,"

I mumbled. Predictably, I felt my eyes start to tear up a bit, and my cheeks flamed. I kept my head down and my eyes on my feet, waiting for Max to start working again. I watched him break up the soil with the claw and tried to keep my eyes focused on the work rather than his forearms. Jessa fidgeted next to me and kept swatting at an invisible fly in front of her face. She punctuated her action with occasional loud sighs.

Max moved on to the rake and quickly smoothed out the row. I was silently begging him to be finished and leave us to it. Whether sensing my discomfort or just impatient herself, Jessa grabbed the broadfork and said, "We got it. Lift, jab, smooth. A moron could do this. Just let us get started. We're good."

I didn't have the nerve to lift my eyes directly to see Max's reaction, but I saw Jessa's. I felt an overwhelming sense of gratitude for my best friend. She knew I was reaching my limit and was trying to get rid of Max so I could relax. I couldn't really explain what my issue was. I was just shy, and I embarrassed really easily. Jessa knew it and tolerated it – most of the time. And, honestly, she shielded me often. Again, she could be a real bitch – even to me sometimes, but she also understood me and tried to help me out when I was struggling.

Max dropped the rake, teeth-side down in the soil. He turned on his heel and began walking away. "You can stop at noon for an hour break. There's a water faucet across the field on the side of the barn if you get thirsty," he said without looking back.

***

Two hours later, Jessa groaned and said, "I'm going for more water," as she dropped the rake to the ground, teeth side up. I nodded without looking up and heard her grab our water bottles from the corner of the structure and walk away. Even though we had been at it for a couple of hours, we couldn't see any progress. Max had moved through a partial row quickly when he'd shown us what to do, but it wasn't obvious in his demonstration how much effort it took to pull the soil up and turn it over. And it hadn't been obvious how tiring the work was. I hadn't expected it to be easy, but the few rows of progress we could see were nothing compared to the space in the greenhouse. If this was our project for the week, I wasn't sure we could finish it with two of us even if we worked the full five days.

Jessa wasn't the hardest worker in the world, but she also wasn't as lazy as her attitude made it seem. We had taken turns doing the most difficult part, which was breaking the ground up with the broadfork. When I was doing that, she would follow behind me with the claw and the rake. Then we would switch. We tried to get through a full row before switching, but we learned quickly that we had to switch halfway through the rows. In two hours, we were only five rows in, and I thought we must have a few hundred more to go.

I grunted as I lifted a particularly stubborn bit of soil with the fork, and then I saw big, heavy boots in the doorway opening. Max looked at me, scowled a little, and then walked away. I felt a little relieved he hadn't said anything about our lack of progress, but then I heard him reprimanding Jessa as she approached the opening, and he followed her in. "Is that your plan? You hit someone's car, put them in danger, inconvenience their lives, and then you let your little friend bail you out? You can't bring her back tomorrow. You are the one who is supposed to be doing this. Not her."

"Jeez, Farmer Max, I am doing this. Maybe you are having a hard time with this concept because I can see you might struggle in the friend department, but Lanie is helping me. *Helping* me. Maybe you've heard of this before? I was just getting water. For both of us. Because this is slave labor. And we were thirsty. Are you okay with that?"

Max grumbled a little more and looked out the opening where his son was playing with a massive white dog. "I came to tell you that my son and I will be working nearby, and you should just keep doing what you're doing in here. I have to check some of the fencing around those fields just to the east side."

"You even make your son do farm work? What kind of dad are you?"

"Jessa," I hiss-whispered, "please shut up."

Max spared me another tiny glance and said to Jessa, "He'll be playing with his dog, Milo, and walking with me. But, yes, he does do some farm chores. Not like you're talking about, though. I wanted to introduce him, so he would know who you are. Save the snark in front of him, and I'll do the same.

"Benji," Max called, and Benji walked into the greenhouse with the dog on his heels. "This is Jessa and," he hesitated as if he didn't want to even acknowledge me or couldn't remember my name.

"Lanie," I whispered, embarrassed.

"And Lanie," he said. "They're working in here this week. Make sure you keep Milo out of their way, okay?"

"Aren't you the lady that ran into our truck?" Benji asked, looking up at Jessa.

"Well, I'm not sure about running into it. Your dad stopped kind of fast and—"

Max cleared his throat and gave Jessa a death stare.

"Hi Benji," I said and approached his dog with my fists closed to keep from scaring him. I was afraid of pretty much everything, but kids and animals were often exceptions. I thought maybe focusing on Benji could re-direct everyone's attention from Jessa being rude to Max.

"What kind of dog is this?" I asked. "He's really beautiful." The dog wasn't wary of strangers at all as he nudged his face into my hand.

"He's a Samoyed," Benji said.

"Wow. Well, he's beautiful. And that's a lot of long, thick fur."

"Yeah. He loves the snow, and he matches it, too! Sometimes we call him Snowball. He used to live where it was hot all the time, but some of Mommy's friends gave him to us because he needed to live somewhere colder. He's my best friend!"

"Is that so?" I asked. "I always wanted a dog. He's so sweet." He was really demanding my attention now, rubbing up against my legs and forcing his face into both of my hands. I looked at Benji and laughed, noticing he looked like a mini Max with his chocolate hair and eyes.

"He likes you! He likes everybody, but he really likes you!"

"Milo! Leave the lady alone," Max said, immediately softening his tone when he looked at his son and saw the dog's head jerk up out of my hands. "She's busy working, so we need to get going." He cut in between the dog and me, and began steering Benji out of the greenhouse.

***

"Oh my God, Lanie. Jet is amazing!" Jessa gushed as we sat outside the greenhouse eating lunch. We had grabbed sandwiches from a spot a few miles away and brought them back, luckily avoiding further meetings with Mr. Parker … Max.

"Yeah? Why does this amazing person need to crash at our place at the moment?"

"Oh, that. That's no big deal. He lived in a house with a bunch of other guys, and the landlord wouldn't let them stay when the lease was up. What a jerk."

"Any idea why this jerk didn't want to take their money anymore?"

"Well, I think they were a bit behind on the rent or something." Jessa rolled her eyes as if this were a ridiculous reason for a landlord to be upset. "And maybe there were some noise complaints from the neighbors. And something about damage to the property, but really, what did he expect? Renting a house to six guys?"

"Right. And what is his plan now? Is he looking with his former roommates for a new place?"

"Lanie, I actually wanted to talk to you about that. I mean, I really like Jet, and I really think it would be great if he just kind of … stayed."

"Like with us? That's what you mean? Move in?" I tried some deep breathing to calm myself. It's not like we had never had this come up before. But not seriously. Jessa fell in love overnight and fell out of love just as quickly.

"Well, with me anyway," she said.

I looked at Jessa, stunned. Did she mean she wanted me to move out? Or that she was moving out? We had lived there together since we'd moved from her parents' house after high school. Even if this went nowhere, it was a shocking conversation to be having about a one-night stand.

Max, Benji, and Milo rounded the corner at that moment, and Milo ran up to me, politely (as politely as a dog could) checking out my food.

"Milo!"

Max's sharp tone got his instant attention, and he backed up a bit.

"Oh, look," Jessa said, "the slave driver is back."

Jessa and I started collecting the remains of our lunch and stood up while Benji asked his dad what a slave driver was.

"Just think about it," Jessa said to me, then spun on her heel and walked back into the greenhouse.

I stood, mystified, looking at her departing frame for a few beats too long. I was so far removed from my surroundings that I jumped when Benji asked if I wanted to play with him and Milo.

Embarrassed at my reaction, I focused on my current reality – helping my best friend out of a mess and working for a man who detested me. I tried to push down the fear that I might soon be homeless, or, at best, looking for someone who had a room to rent. It would be next to impossible to afford a place by myself. That's why Jessa's name was on the lease. It was her parents who had helped pay the deposit to get us in years ago, and they hadn't wanted me on the lease. Even though I paid more than my share of rent every month, it was Jessa's apartment, and she could do what she wanted with it.

Max cleared his throat uncomfortably, and I looked up at him briefly. "Are you okay?" he asked. "Is it too hot or something? Or too cold or …"

I shook my head. "I'm fine. Sorry. Just distracted for a minute." I started to walk back to the greenhouse.

"You can take more breaks if you need to. Don't make yourself sick or anything," he said. I couldn't tell if he was concerned or irritated.

"I'm fine. Really. Sorry. I'll get back to work." I patted the top of Milo's head, who had sidled up to me when I stood, and I gave a little smile to Benji before turning to go back to work.

Chapter 3

I woke up in the little cottage early – disoriented and wondering why my bed felt strange. It had to be before six am. It was quiet and still, and faint light streamed in through the simple but dainty white curtains on one of the two windows in the room. I re-oriented myself, reminded that I wasn't in my apartment anymore. I still couldn't believe what had happened over the last week and how I'd ended up here.

Day two had gone much like day one working at Max Parker's farm. It had become clear to me that he had just given us busywork in the greenhouse as there was no way we would finish it. I had seen his little tractor in another greenhouse, tilling up the soil there within a half hour, and I was quite certain that tractor would be in our greenhouse the minute we left for good. Still, it didn't prevent him from continuing to monitor our progress or show his displeasure with Jessa. He continued to ignore me and, if he had to talk to me, he did it indirectly through Jessa. I felt him watching me a few times as I worked, but I had no idea what he was watching for. My progress? Whether I was getting ready to pass out in his greenhouse and cause him a problem? He had seemed pretty worried about that the day before when he'd caught me dazed after what Jessa had sprung on me.

Jessa had acted like her suggestion was no big deal. She'd clarified on the drive home that Jet would have a really hard time finding a new place, and that they needed some privacy. She thought I would have no problem finding a nice place to rent on short notice, and she promised to help me.

I wasn't intentionally giving Jessa the silent treatment, but I just felt speechless. I had experienced Jessa's thoughtlessness frequently, but I had never felt so completely disregarded or unimportant to her. She was the closest thing to a rock that I had in my life, and it was a miracle that I had learned to have as much trust in her friendship as I had. This definitely felt like the final trust lesson for me – no one had my back but me.

It shouldn't have taken this long to learn the lesson once and for all.

We had gone through day two working in periods of long silence punctuated by moments of Jessa telling me to either stop being a baby or to please not be mad at her over a guy.

Toward the end of day two, I had been taking a quick break just outside the greenhouse after having gone to refill our water bottles. I stopped to take a quick moment to myself before having to go back in and finish off the day's work with Jessa. Milo had come running around the corner and made a comically quick stop when he saw me. He sweetly cocked his head to one side and then slowly approached. I felt tears prick my eyes as I reached my hand out to the dog. He tucked his head under my outstretched hand, and I bent down to really give him a good rub and take some comfort from his sweetness.

Benji rounded the corner next, and his motion wasn't very different than his dog's had been. "Hi," he said to me as he came up and put his hand (with just a touch of possessiveness) on Milo.

"Hi Benji." I wanted to say something else to the adorable little boy, but I was fighting tears and didn't want to lose it. I kept my head down as if Milo's fur were the most interesting thing in the world.

"Are you sad, Lanie?"

I began to shake my head when I heard Max's sharp voice. "Benji! Leave the lady alone. Let's head inside and clean up."

"Bye, Lanie. Lady Lanie!" Benji sang as he skipped toward his dad.

"Alright?" Max curtly asked with a glance at me.

I nodded and turned to go inside.

Day three was when it had happened. I had just parked outside Max Parker's house, and Benji had run out toward my car as Jessa and I were getting out. "Lady Lanie, Lady Lanie!" Benji called. "You're here! I want to show you Milo's new trick! He spins for his treats now. I worked with him all night and now he can do it. It's so cool!"

I smiled at Benji, who was practically spinning around himself in his excitement. "I'd love to see that, Benji. Nice job training him!"

Max was approaching during this conversation, and as he got closer, Benji turned to him and said, "Dad, what about Lady Lanie? I bet she could do it!"

"Benji, leave Lady— I mean, leave Lanie and Jessa alone. They're here to finish their work and then they'll be leaving at lunchtime today. You can show them Milo's trick later this morning when we're out by the greenhouses."

Jessa slammed the door and stepped toward Max while asking, "What could *Lady* Lanie do? What's he talking about?"

"Nothing," Max said as Benji talked over him: "Lady Lanie could be my babysitter and the cooker and the cleaner! Mrs. Harris used to do it, but she had to move closer to her daughter last year, and now Dad has to find someone new before all the new workers come in. Dad, she could do it! Milo likes her, and I bet she knows how to cook real good."

Clearly, Max hated this idea. I tried to quickly get us all out of the awkward situation as I explained to Benji. "That sounds like a lot of fun. Anyone who gets to spend time with you will be lucky, Benji, but I have a job. I can only be here this morning and then I have to go back to my regular job. I'm sure you'll find someone as nice as Mrs. Harris again."

"I hope not. I mean, I hope someone nicer. Mrs. Harris was scary. But you're not scary and you fit here and you would get to live here and see me and Milo every day!"

"Benji, that's enough. Jessa and Lanie need to get to work, and we need to do some morning chores," Max said in a firm voice, indicating the discussion was over.

Jessa didn't care what Max's voice indicated and said, "Live here? What do you mean, Benji? Did Mrs. Harris live here?"

"Yeah, she lived in our spare room during the season when the workers were here. She made the farm meals for everybody and cleaned the house and took care of me and Milo when Daddy had to work. But now Daddy says the new person will stay in one of the intern cabins."

"Intern cabins?" Jessa asked with an eyebrow raised at Max.

Max sighed, already understanding Jessa enough to know it was easier to explain things so we could all move on. "The college has an agricultural program, and they place interns here during the main growing season. I have some cabins on the property, so I provide the room and board, and the college provides their stipend. I have to have someone help with the meals for them and help around the house. That's it. I'll find someone and, as your friend said, she has a job. Time for us all to get to work. You're both free to leave at lunch. Here's your license back," he said, holding it out to Jessa. "I hope you learned something from this. I guess I'm not holding my breath, though. It was probably a waste of time for all of us."

He dropped his hand to Benji's shoulder and guided him away from us back toward his house. "Bye, Lady Lanie," Benji sadly called.

"This is it! This is it, Lanie! This is perfect," Jessa practically squealed.

I ignored her, grabbed my water bottle from the car, and walked toward the greenhouse. Our progress there was still minimal. We had gotten quicker and a little more skilled at our work, but it had barely made a dent in the greenhouse, despite two full days at it.

"Lanie!" she called, catching up to me. "This is perfect. It's a solution for both of us and it's perfect for you. You'll have a place to live, and you know you love cooking more than anything. If your stupid boss would ever let you add to the menu at the coffee shop, that would be one thing, but your talents are wasted there. And you did that after-school daycare thing for the little kids when we were in high school. You could cook for the interns and take care of Benji *and* have a place to live."

She said all of this in a way that sounded so pleased with herself – as if she were only thinking of me and my happiness. She didn't say the ugly truth out loud – that she wanted me out, and to achieve that, she was willing to put me in some farm cabin for the summer with nowhere to go and no job after, spending a summer with a man who hated me (and would never hire me anyway). Somehow, in her mind, it was suddenly my dream to live on a farm and be a babysitter.

Halfway through the morning, Jessa had gone for water, and I had tried to wrap my mind around how easy she was finding it to kick me out. I was used to her coming first in pretty much everything, but I was also used to her looking out for me and valuing our friendship. She often ditched me for a guy; in fact, she often was short on rent or time or any number of things because of a guy, and it negatively affected me. But this was new. Her kicking me out the door and offering me up to Max Parker to live in some cabin was raising her selfishness to new heights.

"Farmer Max is an idiot. You would be great working here. He flat out refused to even consider you for the job," Jessa whined as she walked back in and set my water bottle down in the corner. "Then I asked him why he even needed someone to do that and why couldn't Benji's mom take care of him, and he got all mad and asked if I had seen Benji's mom around. How do I know if his mom is around? What a jerk."

"You talked to him again? Do you really want me to leave that much? I agreed to let Jet stay. Why do you have to kick me out? What is going on?" For the most part, I hadn't said much to her about it, but at that moment, my anger that she would do this was outweighing my intense sadness. The night before, I had hidden in my room and cried like the baby I was. Jet had the night off, so Jessa had been wrapped up in him and had left me alone.

"Jet likes to live a certain way. He wants to have people over after work, and we know you'll complain about the noise. He wants to spread out more in the apartment. And we just need our space, Lanie. It's time to grow up. We're not kids anymore. Time to leave the nest."

"The nest?" I practically screeched, beginning to stab at the soil more forcefully. "You think I've been living in a secure nest all this time, and I need to spread my wings? Is that what you think?" I threw the claw down and picked up the rake, feeling light-headed as I straightened up and began working again. "That having my mom leave me on my own when I was fifteen and having to move in with your family or be homeless was a nest?" The dirt was kicking up as I punctuated each statement with a hard slap to the ground. "You think working since I was fifteen to contribute and then paying my way since we moved out at eighteen – and paying some of yours at times, might I add – has been me chilling in a cozy nest? Good to know. I didn't realize you thought it was time for me to challenge myself and grow up."

Jessa started to speak, but I cut her off, hurting my hands a little as I pounded the rake into the ground. "Tomorrow. I'll be out tomorrow."

"Lanie, it doesn't have to be tomorrow! I'm going to help you find somewhere." Jessa picked up the discarded claw from the ground. "That's what I was trying to do with Farmer Max, but just because that's not the answer doesn't mean I won't help you find somewhere else. Stop being dramatic." Jessa actually rolled her eyes.

"Dramatic?" I gasped.

We both turned quickly as we heard Milo bark. We saw Milo, Benji, and Max standing in the doorway watching us. Max was scowling.

Great, I thought. Just great. Exactly what I needed to make this even worse. An audience that included Max Parker.

"We're working," Jessa said to Max. "Just a water break. No need to supervise the last few hours. Obligation fulfilled as of noon today. And not a second too soon."

Max put his hand on Benji's head, directing him to turn and begin heading toward the house. I could hear Benji telling his dad that he wanted to show me Milo's trick, and Max telling him now wasn't a good time.

Shame washed over me, and I just wanted to disappear. Jessa had been my lifeline when my mom had left me. We were already friends, and I spent time at her house, but when my mom left and I couldn't pay the rent the next month, I literally had nowhere to go. I had already started my job at the coffee shop even before my mom left because money was always a problem, but I was never going to get enough hours to keep the apartment.

Jessa had been at my house often enough to know my situation with my mom, and she'd known when my mom left for good. She started having me "sleep over" once I had to move out of the apartment. Her parents had tolerated me but nothing more. I'd never felt anything like affection from them, but, eventually, it had become clear to everyone that I had nowhere to go. No one told me to get out, so I just stayed, trying to keep out of their way and cost them as little as possible so they wouldn't kick me out. Affection or not, I was grateful to them.

But this felt like the end of that road. Jessa was done being my last support, and I should have never learned to rely on her. The fact that Max got to see that he was right about my friendship with Jessa was the icing on the cake.

In those last few hours working in the greenhouse, Jessa kept trying to pick up the conversation again, wanting to assure me she would help me find something and that she wasn't actually kicking me out. I was so done. I was ready to get home, pack, and have a minute to myself to think about where I was going to go. I had a little money saved. I tried to be as careful as I could with money because who knew what could happen? But my modest savings were routinely depleted when Jessa was short on rent or needed a loan. At least, she called them loans, although my understanding was that loans were repaid at some point, and hers never were.

As we had been approaching my car to leave the farm for the final time, Max had come jogging toward us. "Headed out?" he asked.

"Yes, Farmer Max. We're all paid up. Have a nice life," Jessa snarked and slammed the passenger door as she settled into my car.

"Lanie," Max quietly said, touching my elbow with just a finger to get my attention before I got into the car. "We could give it a try. I do need someone next week, and I don't have any good leads yet. Jessa says you can cook and that you've worked with kids. And I know Benji likes you. That's pretty much the job. A little cleaning in the house would help, too. The season goes till the beginning of September when the students start classes again. You'd have housing and the job until then."

"Um, thanks," I said as I looked at the ground. My cheeks flamed, and I took a deep breath. I had to say something, but what I really wanted to do was disappear. "That's really kind," I said to my shoes, "but I have a job, and I'll still need a job and a place to live in September. This isn't your problem, and I'll sort it out. No need to worry about it. I'm totally fine, and I'm sorry you heard all that. It's not really as bad as it sounded. I was just upset."

"So, keep your job. The coffee shop, right? Can you cut your hours enough to keep the connection and go back to it full time in September? That would buy you some time. And it's solving a problem for me too. I'll be busy with the students starting on Monday. It's not fair to Benji if I don't have something in place by then." He was looking directly at me as I glanced up at him. It was disconcerting having his focus on me instead of having him ignore me. "Come back Sunday night. We'll set you up in the little cottage near the house, and you'll start Monday morning. Hand me your phone."

I looked at him blankly.

"Your phone. Hand it to me for a second." His brown eyes seemed sincere. No trace of the impatience or irritation I had become accustomed to.

I knew he intended to put his number in it if he was asking like that. I didn't know how to respond to his offer, so I just unlocked my phone and handed it over.

He typed for a minute and then handed it back. "There," he said. "I just sent a text to myself. Now we have each other's numbers." He looked toward the house where Benji had opened the side door to see what was holding up his dad. "I'll expect you Sunday night around seven. But you have my number if anything changes. Good?" He nodded his head once encouragingly.

I hadn't said anything at all. I really needed to get home and think. Everything was just too much, and I felt like I was in a daze. I had gotten in my car and driven away, ignoring Jessa's questions about what Max had been talking to me about.

And now, waking up in that little cottage a few days later, I was terrified I had made a disastrous decision.

I felt paralyzed, but I forced myself out of the soft bed to go face the dragon and his son.

Chapter 4

"Hello?" I called softly as I knocked on Max's side door.

He had shown me the house very briefly when I'd arrived the night before. My cottage was behind his house on a little trail through some thin woods. You could see it from his side door. Deeper into the woods, there were two bunkhouses where the student interns stayed. My cottage was one room that had a full-sized bed, a dresser, some hooks instead of a closet, a tiny bathroom, and a kitchenette area. It was sparse and utilitarian, and I absolutely loved it. It had simple things, but they were pretty and delicate. There was a soft yellow quilt on the bed, lacy white curtains, and the pine floors and walls had been recently scrubbed down. Max had shown me the portable electric heater that I still needed to use for a while. It wasn't quite mid-May, and it still got cold at night.

I wouldn't say I had gotten a tour of the house the night before. Max had just brought me in the side door where there was a mud room that connected to a big farm kitchen while he said, "Here's the house." He'd then carried my two bags down the trail to the cottage and said, "Here's the cottage," followed by things like, "Here's the heater." He told me that we would have some time to check in the next day since the students would only be coming in the late afternoon to get settled. The only other thing he mumbled to me when Benji was distracted with Milo as we stood outside my cottage was, "By the way, Benji's mom ... She died. Passed away. He was just a baby and doesn't remember much. I just thought you should know in case it comes up."

I had thought maybe he was divorced, but to have lost a wife ... his child's mother – so heartbreaking, and I didn't know what to say. I muttered the obligatory, "I'm sorry," and bowed my head so I wouldn't have to see his expression any longer. I'd sometimes wondered whether life would have been easier to have had no mother than the mother I had, but knowing Max and Benji had lost that completely... and knowing that she had to have been perfect because Max and Benji were so perfect ... It was unimaginable. Everything about this was too much, and my anxiety level continued to climb.

"Hello?" I knocked again. I heard Milo belt out a bark as he rounded the corner through the kitchen to reach the door. He put his front paws up and looked at me through the window.

Benji followed, wearing Batman pajamas, and opened the door for me. "Lady Lanie! You're here!"

"I am. How are you and Milo today?" I asked as I gave each of them a pat on the head.

"Good. Can we do tricks today with Milo? Can we teach him something new together?"

"Sure. Of course we can, as long as we have time. Let's see what your dad needs us to do today, okay?"

"Yeah, okay. He's at the computer. I'll show you. Come on."

"Dad!" he yelled as he ran. "Lady Lanie's here!"

Benji led me through the kitchen and the living room to a small alcove on the other side. Max was wearing sweatpants and a T-shirt, and sat in front of a laptop with a cup of steaming coffee next to him.

He looked a little embarrassed to be found as he was – relaxed, still looking a little sleepy and unguarded. He hadn't shaved yet this morning, and I could see the shadow of dark stubble. His expression was a little hesitant – not really friendly but more open than I was used to from him.

I was embarrassed, too, because I had no idea if I was doing the right thing showing up so early this morning. I wanted to make sure I was ready when he was, and he'd always been out the door with Benji when Jessa and I had arrived the week before at eight o'clock. I thought I might have been expected to help with Benji before that, so this morning I showed up at his door at seven-thirty.

"Good morning," we both said at the same time.

"Um, sorry if I'm too early. I thought you might want some help with Benji. I can come back later if that's better?"

"No, no. It's fine. It's great. Thank you. I was just trying to take care of some paperwork before the students come in, but Benji needs breakfast, so I can show you everything while I get that ready." He pushed back from his table and stood. "And we can talk about what you'll need to do. Is that all right?"

"Yes, of course. Whatever you want. But I can make his breakfast if you just tell me what he usually eats. I can have him show me around."

"Yeah?" he asked, working to catch my eye while I was trying to focus on anything but him.

I nodded my assurance, and he asked Benji to show me around. "He can have anything he wants," Max told me. "But feel free to keep it simple. He has a few boxes of cereal he likes in the pantry. Make sure to have something yourself. There's coffee made. Help yourself."

"Thank you," I said. "Let's go, Benji."

Benji had been hopping from foot to foot during this interaction and moved like a dart to the kitchen as soon he knew we were on our own.

***

Max's kitchen was a combination of old and new. It was clearly a farm kitchen, and there were corners of clutter. There were stacks of mail, papers, and various odds and ends that didn't belong in the kitchen – like wrenches and spare lightbulbs. But the kitchen was clean and generally in good order. It had modern appliances and a stocked fridge and pantry.

Benji was loving his job of showing me around, and he pointed out important things like a patched-up hole in the pantry where a mouse had gotten in over the winter and where Milo's food was stored. He had said cereal was fine when I asked what he wanted for breakfast, but when I told him I was happy to cook him something if he'd like, he asked if I knew how to make French toast. I peeked in the fridge and saw eggs in a basket, fresh milk, a jar of maple syrup, and a loaf of bread, and told him, "Absolutely! Benji, do you want to be my helper with this? We can make French toast and scrambled eggs. Would you like that?"

He ran to another part of the house and brought back a step stool that he positioned next to me at the counter. I cracked eggs, sliced bread, and created a prep station. I showed Benji how to dip the bread in the egg mixture, and he took his job very seriously. Hoping Max really was okay with me drinking the coffee, I had sipped on a cup while Benji and I cooked and then started a fresh pot.

Within twenty minutes, we had a stack of French toast, a bowl of scrambled eggs, coffee, and orange juice settled on the small kitchen table.

"Dad!" Benji yelled while I debated how many plates we needed. I didn't know if Max expected me to eat with them or if he would keep working and expect me to eat with Benji. I decided I would put two plates down and wait to see what he did. I was ready to let him know I would come back when they were finished if it looked like he planned to sit down.

Max shuffled into the room with his coffee cup and seemed surprised to see the food on the table. "Wow, this looks great," he said.

Benji stood next to the table, hopping from foot to foot again, the happy energy he had needing some release. "Lady Lanie and I cooked French toast. Come on, Dad. It's gonna be great! I did so good a job. Lady Lanie told me so."

Max took in the two plates I held and grabbed a third from the cabinet before walking to the table. "Lanie," he said, "come join us."

"Dad, I dragged the bread in the eggs! Lady Lanie showed me how and then when she put the bread in the pan, the butter popped up and Lady Lanie jumped and shoved me off the stool. It was so funny!" Benji piled toast on his plate and poured syrup over the stack.

Max looked up at me and gave me a nod, indicating that I should come sit with him and Benji at the table. "Thank you for this. It's really amazing. I won't tell you to stop cooking things like this if you'd like to, but it's also fine to keep it simple when it's just Benji and me." His plate looked a lot like Benji's as he reached for the orange juice. "My days can be pretty long during the season. If you can be available Monday through Friday until about six in the evening, I'll do my best to give you long breaks throughout the day. I just can't say when the breaks will be. I know that makes it tough to plan. But I'll definitely take care of things over the weekend, so you'll be free then. Did that work out with the coffee shop? Were they willing to let you reduce your hours and schedule?"

"Yes, I worked it out. I'll work full days on Saturday and Sunday and be available to cover evenings during the week if they get desperate. I'll tell my boss I won't be able to get there until six-thirty if it's during the week."

"Ah, shit, I'm sorry," Max said as he rubbed his hand across his face.

"Dad! Language!" Benji yelled. "I'm gonna tell Grammie!"

"Sorry, Benj. You're right. Give me a break this time and leave Grammie out of it. I just forgot. Okay?"

"Grammie will start the swear jar again if you keep forgetting."

"I know, bud. I'll remember." Max cut his eyes to me and grinned sheepishly. Then, suddenly remembering what he had been saying before, his expression changed again. "Lanie, this wasn't fair to you. It was my idea to keep both jobs, but that's really too much. I guess I pictured you working a few hours there, not all weekend after long days here all week."

"It's fine. It's great, actually. I'll be able to save extra while I'm here, so I'm ready to rent somewhere on my own when I leave."

"I promise I'll try to give you some breaks during the week when I'm working on something I can do with Benji." Max shook his head a bit and then took a healthy bite of eggs. "This is really good," he said, reaching for his coffee.

"So, other than hanging out with Benji, what else will I need to do? What about cooking for the students? Um, what do I need to know about that?"

"They'll be on their own for breakfast and dinner. They can use the farm eggs and produce, and I stock their pantries with dry goods and other staples. The bunkhouses have kitchenettes like your cottage. But we provide them with a prepared farm lunch every day while they're working. That will be the biggest chore you have. We try to use as many of our own ingredients as we can. The rest we get from a few other farmers or from the County Food Cooperative – the 'Co-op.' We only do organic veg and eggs on our farm here. We get our milk, cheese, and yogurt from Smith's Dairy, and the Co-op is where we get almost everything else."

"Any special diets I have to think of?" I was pretty used to lots of preferences and needs from the coffee shop.

Max looked at me approvingly. "You do know food." He topped off my cup of coffee and then did the same with his. "I'm clear with the college – so they will be clear with their students – that we aren't a vegan farm. We have chickens producing eggs that we eat and sell. But, because we're an organic vegetable farm, we do get a lot of interest from students who are vegetarian or vegan. It helps if we have an option for both at each lunch. Luckily, we don't have any allergies I've been told about this season, so that helps make things easier. I'm fine with mostly meat-free meals, but they don't have to be. The students all know the environment. It's really up to what you want to cook. As long as it's veg-heavy from the farm and offers some variety, we'll be good."

I was reaching my limit of pushing myself to engage in conversation with Max. Social interaction was hard for me – especially with a man like Max. I wanted him to leave, so I could process my surroundings and the things I would be doing. But I still needed to know more before I could get away from this new calm Max I was faced with. He wasn't anything like the angry man I had seen when Jessa and I had been working. He was just being a normal, nice farmer dad who had given me a job and a place to stay. It was unsettling, and I wasn't sure if I would keep seeing this Max or the other one – the dragon – once we left the breakfast table.

"Mrs. Harris made that yucky egg salad all the time." Benji pulled my attention back to the present and my eyes up from my hands in my lap.

Max put another piece of French toast on my plate and said, "Yeah, Mrs. Harris was really a cleaner first, a cook second, and a babysitter last. I actually wouldn't mind if you reversed that order."

Hmm. So, Benji would be my priority, and he hadn't been the priority before. I managed to smile at Max. "I think that sounds good."

"She left a list of lunches if that would help you get started. You don't have to make what she did—"

"No egg salad!" Benji cut off his dad.

"Um, how should I balance …" I trailed off, uncertain how to ask how I was supposed to manage taking care of Benji and cooking at the same time. I wanted to ask if Benji was allowed to help me, but I didn't want to undermine Max in front of him if he saw it differently.

"Benji can help with the lunch," Max answered, understanding my dilemma.

"Yeah, Lady Lanie, I'll help. Like with the toast!"

"But, if the *helping* doesn't work out," Max gave me a knowing look and tilted his head toward Benji, "just let me know and we'll sort it together."

"Okay. Thanks. I'll just start cleaning this up now if that's okay. Benji, do you like to color? Do you want to do that while I clean up?" I pushed my chair out and started collecting dishes to take to the sink, grateful I had the experience of my high school second job at the aftercare program to draw on. I knew enough to keep kids busy.

Max put his hand lightly on my arm, pushing it down to put the dish back on the table. "How about we do this? How about Benji and I clean this up and let you have a few minutes to yourself back in your cottage? Or a walk around the farm. Whatever you need. Here's the list of meals Mrs. Harris left," Max said, pulling out a piece of paper from a drawer near the sink. "You can take a look at that and have the morning to think about what you'll need for this week. There will be eight students moving in later today. They won't need lunch, but it would be great if we could set up a sandwich station for them since I don't want them to have to sort out dinner on their own tonight. There are some long tables and benches on the far side of the barn, and that's usually where we serve the meals. There's also an extra refrigerator and a big sink just inside the barn on that side. I already put sandwich supplies there. Take a look around. Think about a game plan. I'll keep Benji occupied this morning, and if you can take over at around two, that would be great. Does that work for you?"

I rubbed my wrist where Max had touched it and looked over at Benji. He was singing a song to himself quietly and making a smiley face in the condensation on his orange juice glass. I nodded and stood to go.

I touched Benji on the top of his head and said, "See you later, Benji," then turned to go but looked back over my shoulder. "Are you sure you don't need my help? I can just clean up quickly."

Max gave me an *I got this* look, and he stacked the plates together. Benji scampered out of his chair and ran over to give me a hug. I was grateful he seemed to like me. I wasn't sure if it would last after the newness wore off, but I hugged him back and brushed a lock of hair out of his eyes. "Bye, Benji. We'll have some fun later."

Chapter 5

I had plenty of experience feeling unwanted and in the way.
Living with an absent and unreliable mother, never having
known my father, and then trying to live basically under the
radar in Jessa's house to finish high school had given me
plenty of experience. On top of that, there was what Jessa's
brother, Ethan, had done to me. I should never have started to
let myself feel comfortable living with Jessa in our
apartment. I really should have known better. I certainly
knew better now.

As comfortable as the little farm cottage was, and as
tempted as I was to relish in something that was only for me
(at least for the next few months), I would not let myself get
comfortable. I would not forget that Max hadn't wanted me
here from the start, and this was a pity job. Sure, he needed
help with Benji, but I was certain he had connections and
would have worked out something more to his liking. I was
determined to keep to myself and out of the way as much as I
could. I would soak up some much-needed affection from
Benji and Milo, and I would work hard. Then, maybe Max
wouldn't regret doing this for me. And maybe he wouldn't

go back to snarling and snapping like he had when I had been working with Jessa.

In the afternoon, I walked back over to the house and relieved Max of Dad Duty, so he could go greet the group of students who were piling out of a college van with their backpacks and duffel bags. I suggested a walk, and Benji showed me all over the farm.

There were six massive high tunnels and acres of fields. There were also forty or fifty chickens, and while I liked looking at them, I did not enjoy when Benji took me into the walk-in coop and showed me how they collected the eggs every day.

Max hadn't said exactly what time he wanted the sandwiches ready for the students, but I directed Benji back to the barn around four-thirty. I had already looked through the fridge and cabinets in the little barn kitchen before picking up Benji, but I did it again, having him help me take stock and talk through a plan. The supplies were basic but charming in their utilitarian way – mismatched plates, bowls, cups, and silverware with a few bigger serving platters.

We decided to arrange the deli meats on one platter and the cheese and bread on another. Max had also stocked the barn fridge with mustard, mayo, fresh lettuce, and tomatoes, which we would put out at the last minute. I asked

Benji what vegetables he liked, and he said anything except beets. I thought we were safe from beets for a while unless Max still had some hanging around from the fall.

We walked back to one of the greenhouses where Max had some greens already growing. We cut a couple bunches of kale, and then Benji and I raided the house kitchen and scored some apples, walnuts, olive oil, and balsamic vinegar (possibly ancient). I also scrounged in the pantry until I found a can of chickpeas, which I would mash and mix with a little oil and vinegar for a sandwich filling in case any of the students were vegan. I had Benji set a timer to see if I could get a quick batch of chocolate chip cookies into the oven within ten minutes. I had a solid recipe I used at the coffee shop, and I could bake them in my sleep. I filled two large baking sheets with cookies, and I grabbed the timer to take with me to make sure I pulled them from the oven before burning. I also grabbed two cutting boards, a sharp knife, and a butter knife, and we made our way back out to the barn.

I chopped up the kale and cut the apples into slices. I gave Benji a few apples slices every now and then, which he cut into smaller pieces with his butter knife. With the oil and vinegar, I made a dressing, in which I tossed the kale, apples, and walnuts, then put the big bowl of salad into the fridge to go with the sandwiches.

It was still only five-thirty by that time, so Benji and I decided to decorate the tables. The two tables were long with benches on each side that would fit at least four people. I wasn't sure if Max, Benji, and I would be joining the students or not, but I decided to set all the places I could at the two tables just to let everyone spread out and have space if we were supposed to stick around.

We put out the mismatched plates and utensils, and then I grabbed a spindle of twine from one of the barn shelves. We headed back into the house kitchen and rooted around until I found some old cloth napkins, along with a big soup pot, a box of tea bags, a couple of pitchers, and some sugar.

There was a gas grill and a worktable just outside the barn. There was also a Coleman stove on a shelf, which I set up on the worktable. We put some water on to boil and planned to steep the tea bags and have big pitchers of iced tea ready to drink.

Benji had been as patient as a four-year-old could be throughout all of this, but I knew it was time to have a little more fun, so I took a pair of scissors, and we went in search of some dried weeds in the spots still recovering from winter.

I didn't have hope of finding any flowers yet, but I was wrong. We found some lovely, long dried grass but also a patch of cheerful blue violets around the edge of the house. Benji helped me as we put together tiny arrangements on top of each cloth napkin and tied them together with the twine.

"Lady Lanie, I like them on top of the plates. Does that look good?" Benji asked.

I looked at him and was generous with my smile, praising him for how beautiful he had made the tables look by arranging them just right. I wanted to hold something back because I already had alarm bells going off in my head about forming an attachment to the loveable little boy. When I had been in high school and worked with little kids in the after-school program, while also working at the coffee shop, I had learned just how dangerous it was on an emotional level for me to get close to the kids. It was hard to stay reserved when many of them were so openly loving and affectionate. But the year always ended, and then they disappeared. It was painful losing that connection. Serving coffee was easier – emotionless.

Benji had gotten cranky just before we started collecting the flowers, and I could tell he was tired. I wondered if he still took naps, and made a mental note to ask Max that evening, so I could try to help him stick to a good schedule. But, even as a tired little thing, he pushed through and continued to drip sweetness. Milo happily followed us and seemed content to be nearby. It was idyllic, which just made me even warier.

"Daddy!" Benji squealed and jumped off the bench to hug Max. "Do you see what we did? Look at the flowers!"

"Hey, buddy. Looks nice," Max replied, scooping Benji up into his arms. "I think you might be a little sleepy, big guy. We probably should have fit a nap in today."

"No way, Dad. Ashley Berger doesn't take naps anymore. I'm bigger than she is. I cooked and decorated with Lady Lanie, and I'm not tired at all." Benji said all this while rubbing at his sleepy eyes with his little fists.

"Ashley Berger is Ashley Berger, and Benji Parker is Benji Parker. It doesn't matter how big you are, buddy. If you get tired, a nap helps. But this all looks great." Max looked up at me while I placed the pitcher of iced tea on the table. "Really, you didn't have to do all this." His tone when he talked to me lost all the affection and sounded almost angry.

The satisfaction I had felt with my effort drained away as soon as he finished his statement. "It was nothing really," I said. "Something for Benji and me to do. He's great with the flowers and decorating. He has an eye for pretty things."

"Yes, he does," Max said, then quickly broke eye contact with me and twirled Benji around in his arms. "The students are on their way up. Do you need anything else, or any help?"

"Benji, do you think you can bring the big bowl of salad from the refrigerator to the table?" I asked as Max stood Benji on his feet.

"You got it!" Benji said, skipping into the barn.

"Um, I did wonder about the expectations ..." I began.

Max looked up from where he was rolling the twine on one of the napkin bouquets between his thumb and finger. "I told you, no expectation like this. The sandwiches are enough. No need to work so hard."

I began not only to lose the satisfaction I had felt with how things had turned out but also to feel embarrassed about the effort we had taken with the table. "No, um, it's not that really. I mean, if you don't want me to decorate or add things to the meal, definitely let me know. I'm sorry if I went too far. I was mostly wondering, though, if I'm expected to stay for the meal, or if I should leave and just come back after to clean up. I can serve, too, if that's something I should do first."

Max's expression changed from curious to amused, but settled on a scowl throughout my rambling. I couldn't tell which Max was coming to dinner – Benji's somewhat friendly dad or the dragon. "I told you that you can do anything you want for the meals. You didn't do anything wrong. And you should stay for the meal. Get to know the students. I'd like Benji to as well. It makes it nicer for everyone if Benji gets to know the people who are going to be around this summer."

"Okay. Thank you for letting me know. I'll plan to stay for meals and if I should—"

"No serving anybody either," Max interrupted me. "Not even Benji. You're not expected to serve anybody anything. We clear on that?"

"Oh, sure. Yeah. Okay. No serving. Sorry."

Max sighed, and it was clear I was trying his patience. He moved toward the barn, and I watched as he rescued the big bowl of salad Benji was struggling under.

***

The students made their way to the tables shortly after everything had been set out. Max stood and ushered them in. I watched as Max shook hands with one of the students who seemed a little older than the others. He had a full beard and wore jeans that looked like they had worked very hard and a Farming Maine long-sleeved tee. Max called him Rich as they shook hands.

He then greeted the other four men and three women, and I thought about the difference in how he interacted with them compared to the reception Jessa and I had received when we'd first come to his farm. It's not that he was suddenly tour-guide friendly, but he was open, kind, and showed genuine interest in the students. As they all sat down, I busied myself putting on water to boil and making arrangements to prepare more iced tea in case it was needed. I wasn't in a hurry to break bread with this large group. While I continued finding small tasks to do, Max got everyone started by passing around the sandwich trays and iced tea. He asked about everyone's major and their interest in agriculture.

I learned that Rich was a graduate student, and he was the group's supervisor for the summer. He had been involved with the farm either as an undergrad student himself or a supervisor for the last four years. I also heard a dark-haired guy with thick-rimmed glasses named Julian explain that, while he was a literature major, his family had a large ranch in Columbia, where he was from, and he wanted to learn more about farming since he hadn't really been involved with ranching back at home.

Brendan was charming enough that he got away with his comment about not really caring about farming, not to mention his admission that he was in it for the free room and board for the summer. The other two boys, Micah and Scott, were sustainable agriculture majors. They had already spent previous summers at dairy and livestock farms.

Cassandra was an environmental studies major, and Spruce was studying outdoor education. They seemed to be pretty close already and talked about themselves as a unit. Keisha was a sustainable food systems major and had already asked Max where he had sourced the deli meat.

As they all started eating and the chatter became more general, I took a seat next to Benji, which was across from Rich and Max. Max glanced at me and then told the group I was Lanie and that I had prepared the meal for them. They all thanked me and then continued their own conversations. I was relieved that I didn't have to actually say anything other than "hi" and "you're welcome."

The undergrad students had all sat together at the adjoining table and eventually the conversation between the tables began to separate. I tried to focus on Benji while Rich and Max talked about the schedule for the following morning.

Rich burst my invisibility bubble when he cleared his throat and asked me, "So, you're the new Mrs. Harris, huh?"

I squirmed a little to gather my courage to socialize, and replied with a simple, "Yes."

"I noticed we didn't start off with egg salad. A step up, right, Benji?"

"Yes! I told Lady Lanie – no egg salad!" said Benji. "She lets me help her too and is fun with Milo. Mrs. Harris always wanted Milo to go with Dad."

"Ah, that's it! I wondered why Milo wasn't following us today. So, how do you like things here so far, Lanie?"

"Oh, um, good. The farm is lovely, and Benji and I are having a good time so far, right Benji?" I wanted Benji to take over the conversation, as he was totally capable of doing, but his sleepiness was keeping him a little more on the quiet side.

"So fun!" was his only response.

"From what I've seen so far," Max chimed in, "we're lucky we found her."

I felt the blush spreading across my cheeks and looked down at my plate. I tried to tamp down how much pleasure was rising in my body at hearing the small and surprising praise from Max.

Benji chose that moment to snuggle into my side, and it wouldn't be long before he was really ready to fall asleep. "Should I start getting Benji ready for bed?" I asked Max. "I'm not sure what his schedule is yet."

"No!" Benji whined. "I'm not ready yet. I want to hang out some more!"

Max smiled indulgently at his son and told me if I could take care of the cleanup from dinner, I was off the clock after that. "I'll take care of Benji's nightly routine. He can be g-r-u-m-p-y about bath and bedtime."

"That's not true, Dad! I'm just not ready. You try to do it too early."

"Can you really spell that, Benji?" Rich asked.

"Yes. He said I'm stubborn about bath and bedtime."

I smiled at Max and Rich, and asked Benji if he wanted to stretch out on the bench for a few minutes while I started collecting dishes. As I stood and untangled myself, he eased himself down onto the bench until he was lying down, and curled his hand into Milo's fur, who had been patiently sitting next to us when he wasn't chasing bugs in the yard.

I started making trips to and from the tables to get the dishes into the barn sink, but I had only finished a few trips before Max stood and said, "Right. Farm rule – everyone takes care of their own mess. Why don't you all clear your plates into the compost over there and then stack them in the sink?"

The students jumped right up, and before I could blink, the tables were cleared. I looked at Max gratefully. I found I was quickly just directing the cleanup rather than actually doing it. I had a sink full of dishes, but everything was cleared and stacked neatly within a few minutes.

I knew it was a bad idea for Benji to actually fall asleep at this point, so I asked if he wanted to come in the barn to grab the desserts. After Max's earlier reaction to the napkins and other efforts, I had been reluctant to present the little bags of chocolate chip cookies Benji and I had made earlier. We'd neatly stacked cookies in small, individual paper bags and tied them with strings of twine with sprigs of red winterberry tied in. Now, since it seemed everyone had enjoyed the meal, I felt a little better about it.

Benji came running in, eager to grab the tray with the bundles of cookies neatly arranged on it. He carried it out and presented it to each of the students for them to pick a little pouch for themselves.

I started on the dishes and could hear the group breaking up just outside the barn. The students and Rich were headed back to their cabins for the night, and I heard they would meet up at eight the following morning.

"Thanks for everything today," Max said from just inside the barn door opening.

I startled a bit and looked up from the dishes in the big commercial sink to see him and Benji looking at me.

"You're welcome. I hope everything was okay."

"I think the chocolate chip cookies pushed it over the top for sure. These are great," he said, waving a half-eaten cookie in my direction. "The kids were all happy to have them to take back with them. I don't know when you found the time."

I didn't like the way I flinched at the word "kids." I knew Max was older than me, and I was a little older than the students, but I didn't know how much older Max was. And I was mad at myself for caring – both how much older he was and that he might see me as a kid.

"It was actually really fun," I said sincerely. If I was honest with myself, it had been one of the best days I'd had in a long time. "I like cooking, and it's kind of special to walk right outside and cut fresh kale. I think we did okay, right, Benji?" I smiled at him, and he rewarded me with one of his own.

"So, like I said," Max began, "I should be good with Benji in the evenings. I'll do his bath and get him to bed. Do you mind planning to be at the house at eight tomorrow to get him breakfast and watch him until after the farm lunch? We should be ready to eat around one."

"Sure, but I can be there earlier if you need me. I heard the plan for you all to get started at eight."

"The kids will start then. Rich knows enough to get them going. I'll catch up with them a little later. Also, after the lunch tomorrow, I can manage with Benji. You could go to the Co-op and the dairy to get groceries now that you know how we work things. I have accounts at both, and they know you'll be coming in and charging to the accounts, so you just need to tell them when you check out. Then you could have the rest of the day to yourself."

"What kind of budget do I need to keep in mind for the groceries?"

"I've never had to set anything, really. Mrs. Harris was pretty frugal by nature, though. I think we can see how it goes and if we need to tweak the process once we get going, we can. Maybe no caviar though, right?" He gave me a little grin to go with his joke.

I just nodded and tried to offer a smile.

"Do we need to put a heater out here? I have some spares. It's going to warm up soon, but it's getting a little chilly tonight."

"I'm fine. Almost done. And I'm dressed for it." I looked down at my wool sweater that was over two other layers of shirts. Together with my wool socks and beanie, I really was fine, despite the early May evening. "Good night, Benji!" I shook the soapy water from my hands and walked over to give him a hug.

"Night, Lady Lanie. See you tomorrow!"

"You good? Anything you need in your cottage?" Max asked as he turned to guide Benji out of the barn.

"I'm good. I have everything I need. All set. Thanks," I said, letting out a big sigh as they walked away.

Chapter 6

When I arrived the next morning at the back doorstep, Benji was waiting. He had on Superman pajamas, and I sensed a theme. He led me to the kitchen, and I wondered whether I would see Max at all. There was still coffee keeping warm in the pot, so the evidence of his being up and about was there, but maybe he would slip out now that I was here.

"Lady Lanie, what are we doing today? Daddy said we only have until lunch, and then I have to help him with farm chores. I want to make cookies again! And I want to go see the chickens so they can chase you again!"

"Good morning, sweet Benji," I said, kneeling down to give him a tight hug. "Why don't we start with some breakfast and then we can make a plan. Sound good?"

I had seen a package of blueberries the day before when I had checked out what they had, so I put some oatmeal in a pot to cook on the stove. I cooked enough for Max as well in case he was still around.

He did breeze into the kitchen, but it was a quick stop. I scooped some oatmeal in a bowl for him, dropped in blueberries, and drizzled maple syrup across the top. He told me again that I hadn't needed to prepare anything for him, but he seemed to gratefully accept the bowl, and took it with a cup of coffee back into the other room, apologizing that he still had some paperwork to take care of before heading out.

As he left the kitchen, I turned to Benji, who was at the table with me, eating oatmeal. "How about we do our paperwork now, Benji?"

"What paperwork do we have? I don't have a computer like Daddy."

"We can do real paperwork – on paper," I teased, and Benji laughed.

I pulled a notebook and pen from a bag I had brought with me and set it on the table. "First, we need a game plan for the day. I'll write out the things I need to do and then you can help me figure out when we need to do what."

We worked through a plan to do some baking first thing that morning. I was going to make some bean and veggie pies and needed to prepare the dough so it had time to rest. Then I wanted to make some kind of green dipping sauce for the pies. We decided we would visit the greenhouses to pick something fresh. We also decided on a dessert. The options were a bit limited until I could get to the store, but we had apples, flour, sugar, and eggs, so I suggested an apple cake. Benji was excited and asked if I would need him to help cut up the apples again.

"What about decorations? Can we do flowers and berries again?"

"Well, we need to do some cleaning and laundry here in the house for a bit first. We need to get those napkins clean after all. As soon as we get that finished, we'll take a walk and see what we can find for decorations. See," I pointed to the paper, "here's where I wrote: 'make dough for pies'; and here is: 'clean house.' This one is: 'take a walk to pick greens and decorations.' Can you draw a picture next to each line, so we'll know what we need to do?"

As Benji was doing his best to illustrate the tasks, Max walked in the kitchen to put his cup and bowl in the dishwasher. "Daddy!" Benji said. "We did paperwork and have a plan-game!"

"Is that right? Well, I'm glad to hear it. Maybe you can help me with my plan-game this afternoon, too." Max picked up Benji and kissed each cheek. Benji showed him the notebook. He looked it over, and, with a quick glance at me, told Benji to be good for me and that he would see him at lunch.

Benji and I set to work once we finished eating. He got a little bored while I cut the vegetables for the pies, but I put on some music on my phone, and we added dancing to our cooking routine. Benji particularly liked a big band jazz playlist I turned on. We did a little dance challenge where we tried to outdo each other. Luckily, this activity successfully carried over into the hour or so we spent cleaning up the house and doing a load of laundry.

I was incredibly curious about the rest of the house, but I wasn't ready to glimpse into Max and Benji's more personal space yet. I straightened, vacuumed, and dusted the downstairs space only for now. I asked Benji to run upstairs and bring down some clothes for the day, which he had to do a couple of times after I bargained with him not to wear thin pajama bottoms outside.

We trekked around the farm with Milo, playing fetch and collecting decorative treasures in an old basket I found. I saw most of the students working in the greenhouse that had recently been tilled. It looked like they were planting seeds in rows. Surprisingly, I saw Cassandra and Spruce doing the work Jessa and I had been doing in the same greenhouse we had worked in. They looked about as happy as we had when we were doing it.

We found Rich and Max looking at a tractor in a nearby field. Benji and Milo ran to Max as soon as they spotted him. Max was really filthy, and frustratingly, I felt my eyes drawn to his strong, grease-stained forearms. Despite the cool air, he had worked up a sweat and had dirt marks across his handsome brow. Max put up his hands as Benji approached and said "Whoa, big guy" to keep Benji from jumping up into his arms. Instead, he leaned down and kissed the top of Benji's head.

"Good morning, Lady Lanie," Rich said. "What are you two kids up to today?" Rich wasn't anything to sneeze at, covered in dirt and grease either, but my eyes kept straying back to Max.

"Oh, we were just enjoying a walk and collecting some treasures. What's going on here?" I gestured to the tractor.

"Clogged carburetor ... we think," he replied. "I keep telling Max he's going to have to stop fixing this old thing and invest in a new one."

Could a person roll their eyes without actually rolling their eyes? I felt like Max did in that moment, although his eyes just moved between Benji and me.

Maybe it was the fresh air, Benji's company, or such a friendly reception, but I felt more comfortable now and could keep up the conversation without feeling like I was going to hyperventilate, so I asked something I had been wondering. I pulled some dried orange pods that were about the size of golf balls from my basket. "Do either of you know what these are?"

"Chinese lanterns," Max answered right away. "But I'm surprised you found any after the winter." He took one from my hand, and I thought it was probably good I was wearing gloves.

"They were under a little eave on the side of the house, so I guess they were able to find a spot to stay dry and protected. They're still so colorful and beautiful."

"There are a lot of flowers and decorative plants that grow on that side of the house. We haven't really done anything with them in a while, but you'll have as many as you'd like to collect soon – along with a jungle of weeds in between."

"Mommy liked the flowers, right, Dad?"

"Yes, Benji. That's right."

I felt the moment stretch – the sad little moment of silence that often happens after mentioning something about someone who has passed away. Max and I exchanged meaningful looks. At least I hoped he understood my meaning – *I'm sorry that happened to you. I hope you're okay.*

Luckily, Rich knew how to break the tension. "We better get this tractor fixed before lunchtime, boss." He picked up a stick and tossed it for Milo to chase.

"What's for lunch today, Benji?" he asked.

"You'll have to wait for the surprise, Mr. Rich, but it's gonna be so good!"

Lunch was, in fact, good. Everyone was starving after a long morning of work, and they ate every crumb. I had found an old percolator in the barn and had coffee ready to go on the Coleman stove burner as well, so they could get caffeinated for the afternoon before heading back out.

"Headed to the Co-op then?" Max asked as I started on the dishes after the interns headed back out.

"Yes, I'm actually excited to go stock up. I need to do a little more planning before I head over, but I have some ideas."

"I didn't expect this, Lanie," he said, gesturing to the sink and back out to the area where we had lunch. "But thank you. You've really surprised me – with Benji and your cooking and … I'm glad things worked out this way."

"Wow," I said, feeling stupid as soon as the word fell out of my mouth. I mean, in my defense, I was stunned by what he said. "Wow" was at least a better response than "no shit, really?" – that one was also rattling around in my brain.

I pulled myself together enough to form a sentence. "From not being able to look at me to being glad I'm here. *I* didn't expect *that*." Was I teasing him? What was wrong with me?

"Is that sass?" he bandied back. "Is there sass under there?" he asked with a surprised smile. And he was teasing me? What was happening?

"Um, yes," I laughed a little. "I do have some sass. I didn't mean for it to come out though. Sorry. I'll be more careful in future."

"What's sass, Dad?" Benji looked between the two of us.

We both laughed at Benji and went back to our own business – Max headed back out to the fields with Benji and Milo in tow, while I finished up the dishes, trying to push down the little bubble of happiness that kept trying to surface.

***

I was worried. My list was massive. My head had been spinning with ideas for these meals. I had been given all this freedom and resources to be creative, and it was exciting, but I was afraid I had gotten carried away. I had already gone to the dairy farm and picked up several glass bottles of milk, cream, butter, and some farmer's cheese. They didn't make hard cheeses on site, but I could get those at the Co-op. I was glad there were no prices discussed at Smith's Dairy. The farmer knew Max and just gave me what I asked for without any questions. I had seen those glass bottles of milk in the store. They weren't cheap.

And now, standing at the checkout at the Co-op with an overflowing basket, I was worried. Would Max think I had spent too much? I was definitely "frugal by nature", as Max had characterized Mrs. Harris. That was something I shared with my predecessor. But, when it came to food, it was hard not to let my excitement for what I could create get the best of me. I had been able to take a peek in Max's root cellar, which gave me an idea about all the produce he had in addition to the greens already growing in his high tunnels (surprise, Benji, you still have beets stored!). I was ready to make sweet potato and bean chili, banh mi sandwiches with pickled vegetables and homemade bread, warm grain and veggie salads, and I had so many pie ideas. I was constantly writing a new one down in my notebook.

"That'll be $212.94," the cashier said to me, bringing me back from my visions of beautiful dishes.

"Oh, right. Um, I'm working for Max Parker, and he said I should put it on his account. I'm Lanie. Lanie Billings?" I said my name as a question, hoping it was familiar to her.

The woman gave me a friendly smile and said, "Max told me about you. No problem. All on his account. Looks like his interns will be eating in style this summer."

"Oh, no. Is it too much? I was worried it was too much."

"You're fine. Mrs. Harris would do something similar every week. Unless this will only be for a few days?" She looked at me with a touch of concern.

"Oh no! Definitely for the week! Hopefully longer. I'm really trying to make the most of what Max already has. I just needed to stock up on some basics to get me started and some fruit we don't have."

"You're fine then. Really. Don't worry. Max is really nice, and I've never known him to be stingy with his crew."

What did she know about his crew? I looked at the pretty cashier more closely as she bagged the groceries into the cloth and mesh bags Max stored by the door in the mud room. She was older than me – maybe early thirties. Certainly closer to Max's age than mine. Was she interested?

Did they have a thing? Was it any of my concern? The answer to that particular question was easy. No, no, no.

"So, you've known him a long time?" I told myself to shut up, but the question came out anyway.

"We went to school together. Grew up together – sort of. My family used to own a farm a few miles from his house. He didn't have a farm back then, but when he finished college, he came back and bought the old Miller farm. Completely overhauled it into organic vegetables. He got into farming as my family was getting out of it. But I ended up running this place, so I see him often. We sell a lot of his produce, and he's a good customer."

What was the appropriate response here to all this new information? *Thank you for the gossip. Can I ask for more?* didn't seem appropriate. I settled on an ever articulate, "Oh, I see."

"I'm Willow. Willow Miller," she said, extending her hand to me.

"Willow Miller – like Miller Farm? The one Max bought?"

"You caught that, did you?" she asked with a sweet smile. "It was awkward at first, but I tried to stay out of it. And we're good now. Max was a few years older than me in school, so it's not like we knew each other well. He was looking for a farm at the same time the bank was … well, at the same time the bank was foreclosing on my family's farm." Her voice wavered involuntarily on the word "foreclosing." She took a deep breath and continued. "It sucked. But there aren't really secrets around here, so you might as well hear it all directly from me. Max tried to keep things quiet – tried to give the impression my parents were choosing to sell. Didn't help that the local banker's family who held the mortgage lacked the same discretion."

"I'm so sorry. That must have been hard for you. And your parents."

"It was. But, you know, it's actually fine now. Farming is incredibly hard work. My parents practically gave their lives to it. My dad ended up working at the Farm and Home Supply store once they stopped farming, and they eventually bought a small house outside town. It worked out in the end. Max is doing it right. Keeping things small but steady. Using the students and solid practices."

She finished loading the bags back into my cart, and I thanked her several times as she was finishing up.

"Are you from around here?" she asked. "Or just here for the summer?"

"Oh, I'm from the area – but not here exactly. I grew up in Beecham. I work at Pinecone Coffee there, too."

"Ah. Busy girl. Well, it was nice to meet you. I'm sure I'll be seeing you again. It looks like I'd love to sample your food from what you bought. Lucky interns, like I said."

"Oh, I hope so. If I could, I'd invite you out sometime." Maybe Max would? Maybe I needed to get used to the idea that this kind woman with a delicate, graceful figure that lived up to her name would be hanging around the farm? She had said she and Max were "good" now. What did that mean? "Anyway, thank you again." I smiled and started to push the cart from the register. "I'll see you next week."

I lectured myself on my drive back to the farm, pushing the conversation about Max and his farm from my mind. I was trying to make sure I was very clear with myself that there was no universe in which I should ever be thinking about Max's strong hands, or Max's kindness to me, or Max's easy affection for his son. These were not things worth my notice. Whether he and Willow were close, whether she was interested in him wasn't my business, but it certainly was a good reminder that Max had endless options if he wanted female company. I hadn't seen evidence of it yet, but I needed to prepare myself for when I would.

***

After successfully stowing the groceries in Max's kitchen before he and Benji had made it back to the house, I settled into my cottage. I made myself a cup of French press coffee and pulled out a chocolate chip cookie leftover from a few days before. I settled myself at the tiny table in front of the space heater and opened my notebook to do some more planning for the rest of the week.

Just as I was deep in the middle of comparing recipes on my phone for Farmer's Cheese Pie, Jessa's number popped up as an incoming call. I debated longer than I should have about picking up. The last few days in the apartment before I moved out had been spent with me giving her the silent treatment and her vacillating between being indignant and apologetic. I wasn't proud of how I had behaved by not talking to her, but it was really my only weapon. Freezing someone out was all I had, and I could use it effectively – as long as the other person cared enough for it to even matter.

I knew I was being childish. It wasn't Jessa's fault I was so attached to her. She wasn't wrong that it was time for me to wake up and realize I should give up on trying to rely on or trust anyone (even her), so I let out a deep breath and picked up.

"Lanie! Hi! How is it? How are you? How is Farmer Max? Tell me everything!"

I wasn't surprised Jessa had decided to play it this way. She was rolling the dice that if she pretended nothing was wrong, I would just play along. And she was right. I no longer had the energy for the silent treatment, and I was short on people who cared about me.

"I'm fine. How are you doing? How's work?"

"Oh, who cares about work? I'm good. Oh my God, so good. Jet is amazing, and I'm getting to hang out with his friends and at the bar and it's just so cool. Steve didn't take it so well when I called things off after the concert, but it made Jet jealous that I went and, oh my God. The sex after that argument. Holy crap! So good."

I listened as Jessa rattled on about her new love and her games and life with Jet. I wanted to know how she was actually doing, but that kind of conversation usually only happened when she was on a low. When she was high like this on something new and exciting, that was all she could see. No meaningful emotions, or anything real. Just a constant high that she was ready to ride until it was gone. And, with this Jet guy, I knew it wouldn't be all that long.

After I gave her the basics of my job on the farm and let her know I was managing with Max, she seemed satisfied that she was all caught up with me. I told her I was scheduled to work at the coffee shop that weekend, and she promised to stop in to see me.

There was still a bit of time before I wanted to make myself something simple for dinner and settle in with a book before bed, so I decided to go out for a last walk. It would still be another hour or so before it got dark, but the evening chill was setting in. I bundled up in layers, boots, and a warm jacket before heading out.

I wanted to avoid running into anyone, so I stuck to the far edges of the farm, away from the greenhouses and the fields I had seen being worked. I thought about how strange it was that I'd grown up within a half hour of this place, but my life had been so different. My experience consisted of a dingy apartment above the greasy Chinese restaurant in Beecham, where I saw privileged college students run the town. Later, I lived in Jessa's house with her family. That was a step up in my living situation, but Jessa's family didn't have a lot of value for anything other than the work they had to do during the day to pay the bills and relaxing in front of the TV at night. Other entertainment included Jessa's dad getting drunk and yelling at everyone – particularly his wife.

When Jessa and I moved out, I embraced that new apartment with all I had. I was so grateful to be in a space that I could keep clean and cheery and feel like I had a right to be in. But none of those places offered this kind of outdoor, life-affirming feeling. I had always enjoyed a good walk, but having the outdoor space be such an integral and beautiful part of daily life was something completely different.

I was starting to turn around and head back when I saw someone across the field had spotted me and was walking toward me. I kept walking, trying to tell myself I wasn't disappointed when I realized it was Rich instead of Max.

"Hiya, Lady Lanie. Fancy meeting you here," he said as he approached and fell into step with me. "Headed back?"

"Yes," I replied. "Just a quick walk before turning in."

"Turning in? It's a little early for that, isn't it?"

"Well, I still have some things to do. I need to have some dinner, and then I'll read a bit and make some plans for tomorrow."

"You should come over to the bunkhouses tonight. Brendan plays the guitar and we're probably going to have a campfire going. It'll be fun. You should totally come. It gets really quiet here at night, and even when the workdays get longer, no one is ready to go straight to bed."

"Maybe another time," I said. "It sounds like fun, but I don't think so tonight."

"So, what's your deal anyway?" he asked, softening his somewhat rude question with a lopsided grin.

"My deal?"

"Yeah, you know. Did you go to college? Do you have a boyfriend? What do you plan to do with your life? How did you end up here?"

"Oh, um, those are big questions, but I guess the answers are pretty simple. I didn't go to college and don't have a boyfriend. And I don't really have any plans for the future. I just intend to keep working. I work at a coffee shop usually. I met Max ..." I stalled, not wanting to explain how we met. "I met Max," I began again, "and he needed some help with Benji and the house and cooking, so here I am."

"Hmm," he said. "Which coffee shop?"

"Pinecone in Beecham."

"Oh, yeah. I know that one. I'll have to stop in more often."

"So, um, what's *your* deal then? What will you do when you graduate?"

"It might be farming. I mean I love it, but I also have an internship during the school year at Farming Maine – they're an organization that supports and promotes organic farming. I would really be interested in working for them. I like the idea of being a resource for new farmers. And that job might be a little more respectable in my parents' eyes."

"They don't support farming?"

"Definitely not. They didn't even know you could study such a thing in college – let alone at the graduate level. They've told me more times than I can count that they didn't sign up to pay for this degree."

"Sorry. That sounds hard. But I guess working here is good experience at least."

"For sure it is. I love what Max is doing here. He really knows his stuff and has some innovative ideas about extending the growing season."

We chatted for a while longer about the farm, but as we approached my cottage, Rich started trying to convince me to go hang out at the bunkhouses again.

"Come on, Lanie. It's a lot of fun. And you don't have to watch Benji at night, right?"

"Really, maybe another time. Thanks. I'm a little tired, so maybe just not tonight." I couldn't imagine why he wanted me there. There were girls already at the bunkhouse who had to be far more interesting to him than I was.

"It won't be too late. Come on. I'll even hold your hand if you get scared in the dark," he said, bumping his shoulder against mine as we walked.

"Rich," a deep voice said. Max stepped around the corner of my cottage. "Man, she said she was tired. Why don't you head on out so she can get on with her night? She has a long day tomorrow."

I looked at Max, confused, grateful …

"Right," Rich said. "Gotcha. Okay then, Lanie. See you tomorrow. Enjoy your night." He turned to leave and muttered as he walked past his boss, "See ya, Max."

"Hi, Max," I said as he approached. "Sorry. Did you need me? Is everything okay with Benji?"

"Benji's fine. Keisha is playing with him and Milo up by the chicken coop. I just wanted to check on you. Make sure you were settling in and had everything you needed." The words seemed fine, but he had adopted the Grumpy Max tone again.

"Yes, oh, yes. I'm fine. The cottage is great. Thanks for checking – again."

"And everything was fine at the Co-op and over at Smith's Dairy?" Max asked, sounding as if it pained him to speak to me.

"Totally fine. I met Willow," I said, studying him a little to see if he had any reaction to that. "She's really nice."

"Good, good," was his only response.

"We're going to be starting earlier from here on out. Mornings will get earlier and earlier over the next few weeks. I'll keep trying to give you time in the afternoon and evening, but I might not be able to give you as much time as today. Tomorrow, we need to start at seven. Is that a problem?"

"No, of course not. I'll be over then."

"Sounds good," Max turned to leave but stopped for a second. "Oh, and Lanie?"

"Yeah?" I responded.

"I'm not running a dating service here. Understand?" His look was withering. Like a disappointed teacher or dad who was telling me I was a disappointment. An inappropriate flirt.

My face flamed, and my stomach churned with mortification. Did he think I was flirting with Rich? Or even interested in him? Why had he gone from friendly and concerned back to grumpy and hurtful? I hadn't done anything! I was sure I hadn't. That certainty wouldn't stop me from going over the interaction with Rich a thousand more times to be sure, but I knew I hadn't been doing anything wrong.

I could either stutter a response about not being interested in Rich, while trying to express my indignation at his insulting and presumptuous comment, or I could keep my scattered thoughts to myself. I clung to my only weapon (my inner ice queen) and silently let myself into the cottage, closing the door behind me.

Chapter 7

I was tired. It was nearing the end of my third week working on the farm, and I had worked full weekends in between at the coffee shop. Max hadn't been kidding when he'd said the days were about to get longer. I now knew that the lull when Jessa and I were working there and during my first week was, indeed, a lull.

Max's farm supplied vegetables to the Co-op for purchase, but he also ran a very robust Community Supported Agriculture (CSA) program. I had never heard of it before, but I quickly learned about it when staff I hadn't known existed started showing up to harvest, wash, and pack greens and winter storage vegetables in wooden crates to be delivered to homes all over the county. Apparently, people "invested" in a season at the farm and got a weekly delivery of their farm share. I learned that the program was more sustainable and predictable than showing up at a farmers' market, hoping to sell everything that had been harvested.

The regular workers joined us for what I now thought of as staff lunch. Benji and I had very busy mornings getting ready for the meal. Luckily, he was interested in a lot of what

I had to do, and he was also used to entertaining himself with Milo when he got bored.

I had been avoiding interacting with Max as much as possible. It wasn't hard because he was doing the same with me. We had officially gone full circle back to our relationship the first week we met. We discussed any details we needed to when I showed up to start the day with Benji, and then we avoided each other. I had begun cooking muffins or scones or some other baked good to have on hand for breakfast, so we could avoid "kitchen time" together in the mornings. I always had something he could just grab, and neither of us discussed it. I put it out in the kitchen, and he occasionally said "thanks" as he took some coffee and a baked good on his way out of the house.

I had one more lunch to get through, and then I would finally have a day off. I only had to work Sunday at the coffee shop, so I was looking forward to an entire Saturday to myself. Despite Rich continuing to be friendly and the others exchanging pleasantries when we would run into each other or over lunch, I didn't really interact with anyone in a meaningful way. And even though Rich had toned down the bit of flirtation he had shown so many weeks ago, Max still watched me around him as if I couldn't be trusted to behave myself, which reminded me on a regular basis how little he thought of me. That he saw me like people saw my mother.

Luckily, I was always either very engaged with Benji or working during the staff meal. Adding the extra mouths to the meal made it easier for me to avoid actually sitting at the table to eat. There was always something to refill, warm up, or finish preparing while everyone was eating. Even though Max enforced the rule about everyone picking up after themselves, I found plenty to keep me busy.

Brendan, the charmer who played guitar, kept up a lively stream of conversation, and the topics were usually about the work they were doing or some light gossip about professors and classmates. I felt like Cassandra, Spruce, Micah, and Scott were pretty much a pack at this point. I wasn't positive they had paired up romantically, but it seemed like it was at least headed that way. Julian was agreeable and got along with everyone. He was always quick to help me if he saw me carrying something heavy to the table, while Keisha usually made things a little awkward with some sort of earnest, activist comment.

I couldn't relate to the group most of the time, and I felt more than a few years older than they were. I couldn't imagine what it was like to live the lives I heard them talking about. Only Scott was from Maine. The others were from places like California, Boston, and New York. They talked about spending semesters in Italy and Ireland, and contemplated whether they would go to graduate school next or maybe travel or do a year of volunteer work before starting a career.

I tried very hard to not be jealous and bitter. I was used to seeing these students in the coffee shop. It just stung seeing close up that life could be so easy for some people and not for others. I didn't mind working – it wasn't that. In fact, apart from the gut-wrenching feeling of Max disliking me, I was loving my work on the farm. I didn't mind that I was tired. Spending my days with Benji, running around the farm, having license to create food with ideal and plentiful ingredients was something I had never experienced. It was just the choices they had and the self-assurance they exhibited that made me envious. They took up as much space as they wanted in this world, and it seemed no one expected anything different.

But, of course, just when you begin believing your own assumptions, you are proven wrong and reminded you should never assume things about other people.

Keisha was doing her usual thing of turning light-hearted banter into awkward seriousness. "You just don't get it," she lectured the table. "The point isn't about how cute the reusable box is for delivering vegetables to the soccer mom in her yoga pants. It's about getting food to the people who need it. Where I grew up, the only food you could get nearby was at the convenience store where cigarettes were more available than food with any nutritional value. It's great to try to make utopia even better, but we have to recognize that utopia doesn't stretch far outside of certain bubbles. We need rooftop vegetable gardens in cities and farmers who are willing to drive into the city for urban farmer's markets – not bougie ones but real ones in inner cities. And the government needs to subsidize it if the farmers can't charge prices that are affordable for the people who live there."

"Nobody's arguing with you, Keisha," Rich tried to diffuse her agitation. "You're totally right, but recognizing the real tragedies in the world doesn't mean we can't care about other less urgent issues. We can care about both."

Keisha rolled her eyes and picked up her plate to take it into the barn. I felt stupid for having made assumptions about all the students. I knew Keisha wasn't from around here. She was a black student in a state that was almost entirely white, but I had assumed she came from a privileged background just like the others, and I had assumed her ideals were rooted in academics rather than a lived reality.

I tried to look busy preparing coffee from where I had been listening as she approached to put her plate in the sink.

"I like the idea about the rooftop gardens," I said to her. "Do you think it could really make a difference? Is there enough space? Sorry, I don't know how much an area like that can really produce."

"It's just one piece of the solution," she said, grabbing a coffee mug. "But it can definitely help."

"I grew up around here, and I lived close enough to go to the store where there was always fresh food, but I know what it's like to have to make other choices. It's not always affordable even for people around here. I hear what you're saying, but I think there are problems here too."

"Yeah?" she said, looking at me for what felt like the first time. "I guess that's true. It has to be. I just get frustrated and say things before I can calm down. Sometimes it feels like everyone around here is just playing at food production and systems. Like putting food on Instagram. What is that?"

I laughed. "Sorry. I love looking at food on Instagram," I said shyly, hoping she wouldn't go off on me. "Don't hate me."

She laughed then as well and said, "Truth? I like it too, but don't tell anyone. I feel enough guilt about it. You should post your stuff there. I'd look. Don't tell anyone, though."

Some of the others came into the barn with their plates then, and Keisha turned to head out. "Catch you later, Lanie," she said as she walked away.

***

"Lady Lanie, I'm gonna miss you this weekend. I don't like it when you go to work at the coffee shop."

"I'll miss you too, Benji," I told him as we took a walk with Milo late in the afternoon. Max had to work with Rich on some fencing and asked if I could look after Benji until around six. "But your dad said you're headed to your grandparents this weekend. That sounds like fun."

"Yeah, it is. Grammie and Grampie have two cats. But they're not as good as Milo. I'm gonna miss him too."

"What kind of stuff do you do with your grammie and grampie? Do they have a big yard?"

"Yeah, I guess, but it's not like here. Their house is big, and I can't touch a bunch of stuff. We don't go outside a lot, but they always take me fun places like the aquarium and the children's museum. And dad's friend Angela will be there tonight when he drops me off. We'll all get to have dinner together. She's really funny."

And there it was. Proof of a woman in Max's life. I hated that knowing he was with someone made it feel like something was wringing out my insides. Having a crush was a stupid, tiring exercise. I kept trying to crush the crush, but, unfortunately, I admired everything about Max – except how he acted around me. My experience with men had set a low bar, and seeing Max caring about his son, his crew, his customers, even his plants – it was difficult not to admire him.

He was trying hard to help me crush the crush, though. His dismissal later that night when I turned Benji over to his care was a strike against him, and it should have helped dampen my feelings. "Thanks for your hard work again this week," he said as he and Benji started heading into his house. "So, you'll be at the coffee shop this weekend?"

"No. Well, yes, on Sunday, but I have tomorrow off."

"Ah. Okay. That's good. But, uh, Benji will be gone, so no need to hang around here. Go out and do … whatever. I have things covered here. No need at all for you to be here," he said, meeting my eyes for a split second. The look in them told me I needed to make myself scarce. "See you Monday morning. Six am."

"Sure, yeah. Six." I felt the tears burn my eyes as he basically told me he didn't even want to see evidence of my existence while Benji was gone. I looked down at my shoes to hide my stupid emotion. "Have a nice weekend. Bye, Benji," I managed to say as I turned to go.

Chapter 8

The next morning, I fumed as I got up earlier than I had wanted to on my only day off. Max had succeeded in ripping away the little peace I had been feeling in the sanctuary of the small cottage. While I had dreamed of sleeping in, writing out some recipes, and doing a little thinking about Keisha's Instagram idea for the farm meals, I now felt uncomfortable being at the farm at all on my day off. I needed to get ready and get out of the way, but I didn't really have anywhere to go. I could have tried to meet up with Jessa, but she was still, surprisingly, going strong with Jet. I had no desire to spend my day with the two of them – or, even worse, with them and his friends.

While I could seek refuge in a coffee shop to work on my recipes and the Instagram project, working at a coffee shop for so long kind of made that lose its appeal. It was hard to relax when I was constantly noticing the flow of customers, how busy the staff were (or weren't if they were standing around), and comparing the coffee and snacks to what we sold at Pinecone.

I finally decided I could start with a little shopping and then maybe spend the afternoon at the beach. Between what Max was generously paying me, still earning something from the coffee shop, free room and board, and Jessa not asking me for money all the time, I was actually saving a reasonable amount. As long as Max didn't decide to fire me, I knew I should be fine to get a deposit together for an apartment in a few months, and I could use a refresh of my wardrobe. I mostly had black pants and shirts for the coffee shop. I could stand the addition of some new jeans and layering tops for the farm. The temperature was getting much warmer in the middle of the day but was still cool in the mornings and evenings. I was also tempted to look at new phones. I didn't know much about photography, but after my conversation with Keisha, I had spent the evening reading about some of the tricks people used for posting food pictures to Instagram. I didn't think my older phone had a good enough camera to do anything justice.

I knew it was likely Max was already out working somewhere. You couldn't fault the man's work ethic. He rarely had any downtime if you didn't count his evenings with Benji. And I didn't, knowing that he prepared dinner, bathed Benji, and got him ready for bed.

I figured I would be able to easily slip away from the farm unnoticed. I was just about past Max's house on my way to the driveway but froze when I heard his voice.

"I know you want to see him, Meredith, but this is a really busy time for us. Maybe you can come and stay in October. It would be a much better time for a visit anyway. You could visit at the height of the foliage, and Benji will only be at kindergarten half-days so you'll get to spend plenty of time with him."

His voice was carrying from just around the corner of his house. I felt stuck, and considered whether to just keep going to my car even though he would see me at that point or go back to the cottage to wait it out. There was silence from Max for several beats, and then he responded in an exasperated tone. "Meredith, I don't look at it that way. I don't think it's helpful to make a thing out of the anniversary. I understand you want to visit the grave on that date, but it'll be a tough time for a visit. I can take Benji to the cemetery then, and we can take some flowers especially from you. Then we can all go together in the fall."

I could hear Max pacing back and forth. "Fine," he said. "Book the trip for the twentieth. We'll make it work. See you then."

"Fuck!" he growled as he quickly rounded the corner and almost ran into me. "Eavesdropping?" he barked, his mouth twisted into a sneer.

"No, no. I was just headed to my car. I'm sorry. I didn't mean to."

I stood frozen as I watched Max stalk back and forth, looking like he was ready to crush his phone. He stopped and turned his eyes back to me. "Didn't mean to? Right," he scoffed and muttered as he began his frustrated stalk toward his door. "She's absolutely everywhere I turn. Around every fucking corner with her fucking flowers and cookies. Space, damnit. Just some space would be nice." He took a final, disgusted look at me, turned the door handle, and stepped into his house.

Maybe I should have had more compassion for what he had just been dealing with – he wasn't actually talking to me (not mostly), and I assumed it was his former mother-in-law he had been on the phone with – but in that moment, I didn't feel any compassion. I felt anger. And hurt. And frustration. And so much embarrassment – I was a bother even when I tried to make myself useful. If my cookies and flowers bothered him … if my simple presence bothered him … I couldn't disappear any more than I tried to on a regular basis. There was nowhere else for me to go.

I walked toward him before he completely shut the door. "Space?" I whisper-shouted. "You need space? Is that what you said? I realize I take up too much of your precious space even when I'm just doing my job, let alone if I stay here a minute too long on my day off." The tears that often threatened lately, spilled over this time. "I'm actually trying to leave, alright? I'm incredibly sorry I wasn't quick enough for you." Max looked back at me, horrified at my outburst. "If this whole thing isn't working for you, we don't have to suffer the entire summer. I'll start looking for somewhere else to stay today. I'll try to make it quick, so you can have all the space you need."

I turned and race-walked to my car.

It wasn't long before I heard him following me, but I was motivated to escape. "Lanie, wait. Hey, I'm sorry. I didn't mean … I don't want you to leave. Hey—"

I slammed my door and started my car. I saw Max forcefully rubbing the back of his short brown hair in frustration as I took off.

Of course, he didn't want me to leave. I was doing a damn good job for him. Even if I annoyed him, I was working hard. Things seemed to be going well on the job side of things.

Why did he have to hate me so much, though? Why did it hurt and feel lonelier to be around people who didn't want you around than to just be by yourself? I dug in my glove compartment for some crinkled napkins to use as tissues as the tears kept coming.

I needed to turn the hurt into pure anger. Who the hell was Max Parker anyway? And so what if he didn't like me around? That was fine. Keisha and Rich seemed okay with me. Benji liked me. How did I keep forgetting everything life had taught me? Make yourself scarce. Stay out of the way. Be invisible. This morning had been another tactical error, and I needed to stop making them.

***

When I pulled into the farm on Sunday night after a full-day shift at the coffee shop, I was dragging. The weekend hadn't been refreshing in any way. On Saturday, I had spent the day shopping and at the beach. I had upgraded my phone to one that someone who had a really nice Instagram foodie page recommended. I had walked and walked along the beach for hours, trying to let my mind go blank. Then, I had finally sucked it up and called Jessa.

I'd met up with her at the bar where Jet worked. We hung out there until late because I did not want to go back to the farm anytime soon.

"Ethan's back," was Jessa's opening comment.

I felt my wounded spirit sink even lower. "Yeah? Just for a visit?"

"I don't think so, but you know my brother. You never know, but I think he's *back* back. He broke up with that Becky girl."

I took a second to try to steady my breathing. "Living at home?"

"Yeah, but he's looking for an apartment. You know with his job in IT, he can work from anywhere. I think he's ready to stick around this time."

"Oh."

"Lanie," she said impatiently, "please let it go. I don't want you to go all crazy again now that he's around. He thinks of you like a sister."

Sure, a sister whom you convince to sneak into your room at night. I wasn't ready to unpack all of this. I would just need to avoid him as I had been for the last few years and hope he didn't want to see me again.

"He asked about you. He said you should come for dinner soon."

I moved my hands from my glass and shoved them under my thighs because I could feel them shaking, and I knew Jessa would call me on it. Ethan was two years older than Jessa and me. In school, he'd been one of the "it" guys – handsome, popular, a good athlete, a good student. He'd had lots of girlfriends. And he'd had me. His secret that he kept even from his own family.

I really needed to move on from this topic. I couldn't process the fact that he was back and asking about me while talking to Jessa. Instead, I gave her an opening she couldn't resist. In terms she would appreciate.

"Farmer Max is a dick," I said.

Jessa let out a peal of laughter and wanted to hear everything. She was an eager listener to my complaints about him, and eventually, once she got going, she made me laugh until my side hurt with her impression of him and her snarky comments about him. She had no idea there had ever been a moment where he had treated me better. She didn't know he was kind and engaged with all his staff. She didn't know he was generous, and interesting, and sweet with pretty much anyone who wasn't named Jessa or Lanie. Maybe it all went back to how he'd met us. Maybe he thought about forgiving me for that and then just suddenly decided he wasn't ready to. Whatever. Jessa hated him, and that was salve for me in that moment, since everyone else I knew thought he was the best.

When I made it back to the farm on Saturday night, it had been close to midnight, and I'd sprinted past Max's house to get to the cottage. Most of his lights were off, but I saw one turn on when I drove up. I also heard his side door open and close as I ran along the path.

Sunday morning, I had almost made myself late for work, waiting to make sure I had seen him head out into the fields before I made my way to my car to go to work. He had gotten a much later start than he normally did.

I had spent the day at the coffee shop feeling miserable and angry at myself. I knew that I only had myself to rely on, and I knew better than to put any hope in other people. On my breaks, I spent my time looking on my new phone for apartments. I was surprised to find a studio I could afford. Without Jessa in my life and with the ability to build up a cushion again working for Max, I was going to be able to rent a place on my own when I needed to. It was a relief, and I wanted to make sure I had somewhere I could go right away if Max continued to be so irritated with me all the time. I loved Benji and the farm – and honestly, I loved watching Max and being near him when he wasn't interacting with me. When I just got to observe him in his glory. Except for how he was with me, he was a glorious person. But I couldn't stand to keep irritating him all the time, and I couldn't take it when he spoke harshly to me. Ignoring me – I was used to that, but I was pretty good at avoiding confrontation generally and wasn't used to someone talking to me like Max had. It made my heart physically hurt. The longer I ruminated on those moments with Max, the more upset I got, and I soon found myself filling out the rental application and hitting submit.

And now, sitting in the driveway on Sunday night, I had to slip by him one more time. I just wanted to get into the cottage and try to get a good night's sleep before the week ahead. I knew I would have to see Max in the morning, and I wasn't looking forward to it. But at least at that point we could just go through the motions. Almost no need to speak to each other at all.

I looked all around and didn't see anyone, so I prepared myself to make a quick and direct trip to the cottage as I got out of my car. While I was shutting the door, I heard him before I even lifted my head.

"Lanie," Max said softly as he approached. "Hey, I've been trying to catch you."

I could do this. Feel nothing, feel nothing. I looked at him and waited, biting the inside of my cheek to distract myself from any pesky feelings.

"I'm so sorry about yesterday. Truly." I was sort of trapped between Max and my car, and he was trying to force eye contract. "I'm sorry about more than yesterday. Lanie, you haven't done anything wrong. Please don't be upset." I kept trying to look at my shoes or just beyond his shoulder, but he kept moving his head to try to get in my sightline. "I didn't mean to upset you. It was stupid, what I said, how I've been acting. I just …" He stopped talking and seemed at a loss for words.

"What?" I asked miserably. "I'm trying to stay out of your way. Just tell me what I'm doing, and I'll stop. I didn't mean to listen to your conversation. You were just there, and I was hearing before I knew you were even around."

Max's hand found his hair again, and he started tugging at the short ends as if he wanted to pull them out. "You don't need to stay out of my way. That was stupid. I was stupid. You are an angel. Really. It's like you were sent here. You're so good with Benji. You've made him so happy. And my crew has never eaten so well. I need you to understand, this is all on me." He walked toward me and hesitantly … tenderly, took my hand between both of his.

"Please say you'll stay. I can stop being a jerk. I really can. I'm embarrassed by how I've treated you. I want you to feel comfortable here. I'm so sorry I've made you feel unwelcome."

My heart was being uncooperative – fluttering and hopeful, and I needed to shut that nonsense down. "Please just tell me what it is I do that sets you off? I hate feeling like I'm annoying you. I've tried to figure it out. If the flowers and cookies annoy you, well, I can stop doing that. I can do things like Mrs. Harris did. That's what I do at my other job. I just do what they want. It was stupid for me to do anything differently here."

"Christ," Max said, dropping my hand and rubbing his own up and down his face in frustration.

"What you said about a dating service?" I continued. "I don't understand. I didn't do anything with Rich." Max's jaw clenched and he worked his hand through the back of his hair. "I'm not interested in dating anyone. I've just been trying to do my job. I promise."

"I know, Lanie." He groaned and reached for my hand again. "You're doing an amazing job. Everyone can see that. I was being … I don't know. I guess … I guess I sort of feel responsible for you."

"Responsible for me?" I hated the sound of that – like he really did see me as a kid.

"I mean, I brought you here, and you're young and so sweet and beautiful, and Rich – I've seen him … go through women, I guess, over the years. I didn't want to see you get hurt."

I looked at him incredulously.

"You're right. Ironic that I didn't want him to hurt you, and I just turned around and hurt you instead. I'm so sorry. Please, please forgive me."

His expression was sincere, his body tense with apprehension. It was ridiculous that he was asking for my forgiveness. Even after how he'd been with me over the past few weeks, I cared so much about him. Thought he was such a good person. And the agony showing on his face, the tension in his jaw and around his eyes, just reflected that.

In my mind, he was immediately forgiven. Of course he was forgiven. I was never actually mad at him. Maybe he didn't know that, but I knew I had only been hurt. Angry, too, but not exactly at him. At myself for caring what he thought of me. Maybe I should have been mad at him, but I couldn't be. I had never met a better man. There was just something about interacting with me that didn't work for him. I wanted to let him off the hook and try to work our way back to something normal. We had to get through the summer, and I preferred to do that without crying every day in front of him.

"Forgiven," I said simply.

"Yeah?"

"Yeah. Thanks. I'm going to turn in now." I pulled my hand away and adjusted the bag I had on my shoulder, indicating I wanted to get past him.

"Sure, yeah. I'm also sorry if you felt like you had to stay away so long yesterday. Please don't do that again if you don't want to. I want you to feel comfortable and welcome here. I'm sorry I made you feel otherwise. I worried about you last night. I'm sorry if you felt you had to stay out like that. I'm sorry for so many things."

I surprised both of us by smiling involuntarily. "Enough," I said, "I don't think I've ever heard that number of 'sorry's before. We're good. Really." *Stop being charmed by him*, I chided myself. *He's a nice person and feels guilt for making you feel bad. That's all. He needs to put you back into your agreeable box. That's all this is.*

"All right," he sighed. "Let me walk you to your cottage."

"What, why? I'm fine."

"Because I should. I should have done a lot of things, but I will, starting now." He grasped my elbow lightly and turned me in the direction of the cottage. We walked in silence all the way there. The sun was setting and there was a small bouquet of daisies sitting on the little steps in front of the door.

"Apology flowers," Max said as I picked them up.

I looked at him and could see in his chocolate eyes what he was about to say. "Don't say it!" I beat him before he could open his mouth. "No more 'sorry's."

"Only because you don't want me to then," he said.

I brought the flowers to my nose to breathe them in and smiled at Max. Everything inside me told me to be on my guard and to stop taking such pleasure from his kindness, but I just couldn't stop the smile.

He raised his hand and tucked a piece of hair the wind had picked up behind my ear. "You'll break my heart with your sweetness." He stroked my check softly a couple of times. "Good night, Lady Lanie. I hope you rest well. Thank you for your forgiving nature. I know I don't deserve it."

Chapter 9

I hated this feeling. The feeling of knowing I was entertaining fantasies about Max that would never be. So what if he'd called me beautiful and sweet? He also called me young and implied I was naïve and inexperienced. I wasn't inexperienced. My experience was just bad experience. And the hair and the cheek thing? Same as patting a child on the head. He was putting me back in my box, and I was wasting time engaging in delusions that it was something more.

I knew I shouldn't lie in my bed every night thinking of all the ways Max had been kind to me that day or wake up every morning and feel excitement about seeing him soon. I knew it was stupid and, more importantly, bad for me. But I just couldn't stop my mind from thinking about him, noticing him, dreaming about him. Stupid, stupid, stupid.

Over the last several weeks, Max had shown me the same attention and kindness he routinely showed all his crew. After the night of apologies, the switch was flipped. He did stop being a jerk to me – just like that. He hung out in the kitchen with Benji and me each morning for a few minutes while he had coffee and something I had baked. He stuck around when I was cleaning up after staff lunch to make sure I didn't need any extra help. He asked about my weekends, whether I had to work or not. He complimented my cooking and how well I was taking care of Benji and the house. And sometimes he could take a few minutes out of his busy day to play with Benji, Milo, and me when we would run into each other on our walks.

I knew lots about him. I knew he was incredibly sexy without trying to be. I knew any sane, heterosexual woman would want his attention. I knew he was a good dad and employer. I knew he was kind. I knew he was genuinely sorry for hurting my feelings.

But, despite him changing his attitude toward me, he wasn't open. I hadn't actually seen him be open with anyone. I didn't know if he got annoyed when Brendan dominated every conversation. I didn't know if he shared my feelings about Cassandra and Spruce (I thought they were spoiled and self-absorbed). I didn't know if he really thought Rich was a player. I didn't know if he was still mourning his wife. I didn't know if he dated – Willow from the Co-op or Angela, the funny friend Benji had mentioned once. All I could do was make guesses because he didn't share any of his actual thoughts or feelings.

I did notice he often got up from the table and found something distracting when Brendan really got going. I noticed Cassandra and Spruce often got stuck doing crap jobs (like turning over the soil in the greenhouse). I knew that he had warned me about Rich. These were things I could look at to try to make some guesses about his feelings.

But I knew absolutely nothing about Benji's mom. There were pictures of her in their house, of course – one at the top of the stairs and one in Benji's room. And, of course, she was beautiful. My opposite in every way. Where I was pale and skinny, she was raven-haired and curvy. I was generally considered to be on the short side, and she had legs for miles. I had trouble making eye contact, and she smiled at the camera full of confidence.

When I had finally braved going upstairs to clean in Max's house the second week I worked on the farm, I saw that Max lived in a simple bedroom that showed no evidence of his late wife. There were no women's clothes in the closet or drawers. He didn't have a picture of the two of them on his night table. No box with their wedding rings sitting on his dresser. Just a neatly made bed, end tables, and a simple dresser filled with Max's worn jeans, T-shirts, and boxers. I knew those things from handling the laundry. It felt very intimate, and it both embarrassed and excited me. I really,

really wanted to peek into the drawers of his nightstand, but I knew I had no work-related reason to. So, I summoned all my self-control to afford him his privacy as to whether or not they were filled with memories of his wife. Or boxes of condoms. That was another possibility. I really didn't need to know either of those things.

But I thought maybe I was about to learn more. Today was the day Meredith, his mother-in-law, was arriving. She planned to stay for five days, and I knew from the phone call I'd overheard that sometime during that visit, they would observe the anniversary of Benji's mom's death. I was worried about the week ahead. Nervous about meeting Meredith and worried it would be a tough week for Benji and Max.

Benji said he was glad his grandmother was visiting, but he didn't show the same excitement he did about his grandparents who lived nearby. Meredith was traveling from Florida where she lived. It seemed Benji only saw her once or twice a year. Since he was only four years old, that meant he couldn't know her very well.

My opportunity to meet her came later that day in the middle of staff lunch. Max had said he would be late because he had to go to the airport to pick her up. The first thing I noticed – Meredith was overdressed. She wore a tan linen pantsuit with strappy sandals. Max led her to the tables and ushered her into a seat that had a place setting for her next to where Benji was sitting. She reached down to hug him, and friendly Benji hugged her back. It was a bit awkward, though. A cold hug.

"Everyone, I'd like you to meet Benji's grandmother. This is Meredith Romano and she'll be staying with us this week." Max went through everyone's names to introduce them to Meredith. We all said hello and knew there was no way she could be taking all of us in.

I had made taco platters that day – something I was regretting now that I had gotten a look at Meredith Romano and her linen pant suit. The crew was happy to engage in "make your own taco" day from the makeshift cutting board platters overflowing with fillings, salsa made fresh from Parker Farm tomatoes, onions, and peppers, and the scratch flour tortillas I had made. The platters had also made for nice pictures for my new "Farm Food" Instagram page. Meredith Romano, however, did not seem excited about eating with her hands.

I hustled into the barn and filled a bowl with mesclun mix, grabbed a fork, and presented the items to the older woman. "In case you would prefer turning it into a taco salad instead," I said.

Max smiled his appreciation. "Thanks, Lanie."

"Yes, well," Meredith murmured as she arranged her napkin on her lap.

I didn't see Meredith again until the following morning. Max did not enforce the "clean up after yourself" rule with her, and he did not object when I took it upon myself to essentially wait on her and bus her place at the table. He took Benji and Meredith back to his house following lunch and, presumably, they spent the rest of the day together.

The next morning, Benji met me at the door as he usually did, but he was in a sour mood. He gave me his usual hug, but he lacked all of his usual excitement, and instead of hopping from foot to foot while he told me some new story about Milo or what his dad had made him for dinner the night before, he dragged his feet as he made his way to the kitchen. Meredith was sitting at the kitchen table drinking a cup of coffee.

"Good morning, Mrs. Romano," I said quietly.

She simply nodded at me and then turned her gaze out the window.

"Would you like anything to eat? I have some blueberry muffins, or I could cook some eggs or oatmeal," I suggested.

"I never eat breakfast," she replied in a judgmental tone.

Right. I suggested to Benji that he run upstairs to get dressed while I did a quick clean of the downstairs bathroom, and we would grab some muffins on our way out. I made up an excuse of needing to get a few things from the Co-op for staff lunch as a reason for an early departure from the house. I couldn't imagine spending time with the woman, and it was clear Benji wasn't enjoying himself.

Benji perked up and asked, "To the Co-op? Yeah!" I hadn't taken him with me before, and I was glad he was excited to go.

We scurried out of the kitchen. Benji ran upstairs, and I rushed around straightening random things in the living room before speed-cleaning the downstairs bathroom. Max was, uncharacteristically, still upstairs, and I wondered how he was coping.

I didn't know anything about his relationship with his late wife, but her mother was a piece of work. I was angry when I saw how sad she made Benji and even angrier when I saw how she ignored him while we were in the kitchen. Max had told her this was a bad time for her visit, yet here she was. And it seemed like she was not interested at all in visiting. I kept telling myself I couldn't imagine what she was going through having lost her daughter. But what about Max and Benji? If she couldn't find it in herself to at least show them some kindness, that excuse felt very thin. My loyalties were clearly with the Parker boys.

After Benji and I had finished, we grabbed our to-go breakfast, and had almost made our second escape from the kitchen, when Max appeared. He filled up his coffee cup and said good morning to his mother-in-law. She at least greeted him with words, which was a step above the reception she had given me.

"Dad, Lanie's taking me with her to the Co-op!" Benji reported. Some of his energy had returned, and he did do his toe-hopping thing as he gave his dad this information.

Max raised an eyebrow at me and asked, "Is that right?"

"I, I mean," I stuttered, "if that's okay. I need to pick up a few things, and I thought he could come along."

Max dialed back his raised eyebrow and let me know that it was fine. He told Meredith to call on his cell if she needed anything and that he would see her around lunchtime. He then grabbed a muffin to go with his coffee and joined us as we left the house.

"To the Co-op; is that it?" he asked once we were outside the house, his teasing tone back.

"Yes!" I answered defensively. "Why are you saying it like that?"

"Well, several reasons, but I guess the first is because it's six-fifteen, and they aren't open until eight."

***

I didn't see a lot of Max or Mrs. Romano over the next few days. They showed up for lunch, but Max was busy trying to cram in his work and deal with her expectations. I did my best to keep Benji happy when he spent his mornings with me, but he was a little cranky, which was unusual for him. I knew that on the third day of her visit, the three of them went to visit Claudia's grave.

Claudia. I finally knew her name. I had wondered many times, but there was nothing lying around the house with her name on it, and it wasn't something I was going to ask Max or Benji. Especially not this week or on this particular day.

When I ran into Max on a late evening walk, it was the anniversary of Claudia's death. He was walking slowly and with his head down – completely out of character for him. In the evenings, he was always home with Benji, and the rest of the time he was busy working or rushing to get to his next responsibility, so I was surprised to run in to him.

We were both near the edge of the farm. It was my favorite spot to walk – on the opposite side of the bunkhouse cabins in a little grassy area that ran between the fields and the tree line.

"Max?" I asked softly, wanting to make sure he knew I was there. "Hi."

"Hey, Lanie," he said in a tone that suggested he had been aware I'd been there all along.

"You okay? I'm sorry about today. I mean – sorry for what today is … if that makes sense."

He looked at me with a tender expression. It felt like he was caressing me with his eyes, and it surprised me in this moment.

"So, um," I said trying to gather myself, "Benji's with Mrs. Romano?"

"Yes, he's watching TV, and she said she could sit with him. Can you imagine Meredith enjoying *Dinosaur Train*?"

That made me smile. He didn't seem sad so much as pensive. Without talking about it, we fell into step to continue our walk together farther away from the house.

"You don't have to talk about it – of course. Obviously, you don't. But if you wanted to …"

"I'm probably not thinking what you think I am," he said.

I looked up to see a bit of a tortured expression on his face. "No assumptions here," I said, plucking a loose sprig from one of the evergreens along the path. "You surprise me all the time anyway, so I learned that early on."

"Well, would it surprise you to know that, while it's devastating that Claudia died, I'm not sorry she's not my wife anymore? I think that would shock most people." He kicked a rock toward the trees. "I know it's taken me long enough to admit it to myself."

I realized I had stopped walking when Max stopped a few steps ahead of me and turned back to look. His eyes searched my face for judgment.

I moved my feet forward again. "No," I said. "I'm not shocked. I'm surprised, but not shocked really." I took a deep breath and unconsciously plucked the needles from the sprig. "My parents didn't die – at least I don't think my dad is dead, but since I don't know who he is, I guess I'll never know. But they left me. And I know that people expect me to still have certain feelings for them because they're my parents, despite what our relationship actually was. But I don't." I looked over at him, afraid now he would be the one judging me. His expression was open – encouraging – so I continued. "I understand that you can mourn the loss of someone but not want to be with them."

We kept walking for a bit without saying anything. Finally, Max said, "I do mourn the loss for Benji. And just that she had her life cut so short. She was packed full of life and had so many dreams. It wasn't fair – it never is, I guess."

After a few more seconds of walking along in silence, he asked, "So if you get it, what's surprising about it then? What did you mean by that?"

"Just ... well," I hedged. "Just, you're so great, and she was so beautiful, and Benji is perfect. And I just assumed your relationship was great. Not that all relationships are great. But that yours was."

"Because who could ever be mad at me?" He smiled at me and continued. "I think you're the first person who could testify as to what an ass I can be." He kicked another rock out of the path. "Claudia and I wanted different things. We met in college, and she knew I wanted to farm. I think she was in denial about what life would be like. She was excited about it at first, but when reality set in ... she wanted more money, nicer things, more people, lots of traveling. She didn't ... She didn't bond with Benji. And it wasn't a postpartum thing. She was resentful of the level of commitment. Those were her actual words. That was the hardest thing. And I'm sure I was an ass, so there's that." He let out a jagged sigh.

"How old was Benji when she died? Can I ask what she died from? But you don't have to tell me. Really, it's none of my business. I'm sorry I asked."

"Lanie, you can ask me anything." Max ran his hand through his hair. "I'm still kicking my own ass every time I think about how I made you so cautious around me."

I smiled and quickly assured him, "You didn't do that on your own. I'm cautious with pretty much everyone."

"You don't need to be with me. I won't do that again. I know you haven't deserved a single thing I've dished out. Not one thing – that was a hundred percent me. And I'm still sorry."

Our hands had brushed a couple of times as we walked along, but it felt heightened now. They touched again, and Max looked at me as he took my hand in his. He squeezed gently as he repeated his apology. Then he continued holding it as he said, "She had a blood flow issue with the arteries in her brain. A problem she was born with. Of course, we didn't know that until later. She got a headache. That was it … the only warning. It was clear it wasn't a normal headache, and we went to the hospital. It turned out she had a ruptured brain aneurysm and within twenty-four hours she was just gone. Just like that. Benji was about a year and a half old."

I felt ashamed that this tragedy didn't hit me harder. I was still feeling angry at how she had felt about Benji, and I irrationally felt angry at her for leaving Max like that when Benji was so little.

"I know I'm a bad person for even thinking this, but I'm glad Benji is surrounded by love and care. I'm sorry for what happened to her and what you had to have … have to still be going through. But that's not right. She was an adult when she decided to marry you, knowing the plan was to live on a farm. She was an adult when she got pregnant and decided to bring a child into the world. It's not fair to just do things and then regret them or feel like it's not your fault you ended up there because you dreamed it would be different. She shouldn't have said something like that about Benji. How could she resent such a wonderful, amazing—"

I was getting a little worked up, and Max stopped walking, tugging my hand until I stopped with him. "Lanie, it's okay. Really. I'm glad you have our backs, but we're good." He looked at the trees behind me and continued.

"Claudia was … amazing. She really was. She was funny and quirky and loving in her own way."

I was still angry but already regretting my outburst. I tried pulling my hand away from Max, but he just gripped it more tightly and continued talking. "I just know I can now admit our marriage wasn't amazing. And I don't know how things would have played out, but I need to separate the two things – the grief over her lost life from the life we were living when she died."

My face burned with shame. A woman died tragically, and I was mad at her and jealous and lacked all the genuine sympathy that I should feel from just a basic human level. I looked down past our joined hands to my feet. "I'm sorry, Max. My feelings are … I'm ashamed that's the way I feel. That's the way I reacted. I know it's not right. I just – I know I'm projecting my feelings and it's not the same thing at all. My mom didn't look after me … made me be the parent. It's not the same thing at all. I'm sure Benji only felt love even then. I'm sure she wasn't anything like my mom."

Max let go of my hand only to wrap both hands around my waist and up my back. He pulled me into him and hugged me. I stood for a couple of seconds with my hands at my sides, taking in the fact that I was a horrible person and, instead of walking away, Max was hugging me. Hugging me. And I was just standing there.

I tentatively snaked my own arms around his solid middle and burrowed my head into his chest, while one of Max's hands moved into my hair and caressed the back of my head, down to my neck and shoulders and back up again. "Sweet, sweet girl," he murmured as he planted little kisses on the top of my head.

I knew I was stupid not to freeze everything out and put up every wall I had, but I took in the smell and feel of this wonderful man and tried to nudge as much comfort and love into his chest as I could give. We hugged for an unnaturally long time. I wasn't going to be the one to let go. I pushed one of my hands into the middle of our hug to lay it flat on his chest, and I just rubbed back and forth right over his heart. I could hear it beating, and I tried to tell him everything I was feeling with my hand as I smoothed it back and forth across his sturdy chest. *I think you're amazing*, my little hand said. *You are the kindest, most generous man I've ever met. I think you're perfect even when you're grumpy.* I stroked and stroked over his heart and said all the things in my head that I truly felt.

Of course, it had to come to an end, and when we finally broke the hug, Max reluctantly said, "I should probably get back. Meredith …"

"Yes, Benji needs you back there I'm sure," I told him. He took both my hands in his and brought them to his mouth. He kissed the tops and then turned them and kissed each palm. Then he took my face in his hands and shifted my face up to look at him. "Is this okay?" he asked. I nodded, feeling the brush of his hands cradling my face. The corner of his mouth hitched in the tiniest smile and his eyes were warm. He reached down and gifted me with the most tender kiss on my lips. It was nothing more than a tiny graze, but I felt it like a jolt of electricity.

We fell in step hand-in-hand again as we walked in silence back toward the house. I had no idea what to say, and I didn't want to risk breaking up the cloud I felt like we were still walking and breathing in. It was what I imagined it felt like to be a bird in the clouds – weightless, beautiful, suspended. I didn't know what any of it meant, but I knew better than to analyze it in this moment. I wanted to soak up every bit of these precious seconds. Of this feeling.

We naturally released hands as we got closer to the house. When we got to the path that led to my cottage, Max turned to keep walking with me, but I told him I was fine, and he should get back to Benji. We looked at each other and I wasn't sure about him, but I was feeling so many things. There was no way I could put any of it into any meaningful words.

"Get some rest," he said as he traced the back of my forearm with this finger. Then he turned away and headed to his house.

Chapter 10

Two days later, Meredith left, and no one was sorry to see her go. Sad, but it was the truth. Benji perked up, and the uncomfortable cloud that had hung over staff lunches while she was there dissipated.

Max and I didn't re-visit hugs and hand holding. There wasn't much opportunity, and I was so confused about how he felt. Were the sweet words and small kisses paternal in some weird way? He definitely had let me know he felt responsible for me. And I had to admit, he was affectionate with me in a similar way to how he was with Benji. Most of the time, I chalked our walk up to it just having been comfort on a hard day. But when I was feeling wildly optimistic, I would entertain the idea that he actually found me attractive and wanted to hug me and hold my hand.

The truth was, I had no idea, but I did know he was sweet day in and day out. He asked me enough about my life to have gotten the story out of me about my mom and moving in with Jessa. He knew the short version from when he'd overheard my conversation all those weeks ago with Jessa in his greenhouse, but he wanted to put the pieces together. He found moments to ask me about myself in the mornings when Benji would run upstairs to get dressed or when staff lunch was breaking up and Benji would run around with Milo. And he constantly complimented me on how I'd coped with what I had gone through and the person I'd become. His concern and kindness sparked a warm feeling in my chest that I wasn't used to. It made me afraid – my experience had taught me not to hope, but I had never known anything like this life I was living on his farm.

My friendship with Keisha had continued to grow, too. She would often sit at our table during lunch instead of with the other students. She liked hanging out with Benji and me in the evenings when her work was finished but Max was still in the fields. I found out she was on full academic scholarship at the university, and she idolized Marion Nestle, who I learned was a food politics guru. Keisha also championed my little food blog I had started at her suggestion. She had spent a few evenings with me in my cottage where I played with some staging ideas for pictures of coffee and various treats I had baked.

I was still keeping in touch with Jessa, but I wasn't really spending time with her. Instead, I was surrounded by a small circle of people who seemed to be interested in me and were consistently kind to me. Sure, most of the students basically ignored me and probably thought of me as the hired help who'd never gone to college, but that was totally fine with me. I was used to that from the coffee shop. But Rich, Keisha, and Max's regular crew seemed to think I was worth their interest, and they were always kind, asking me about my next culinary creation as if I were doing something special.

Keisha and I had been talking for weeks about a beach day together, and it finally happened in mid-July when I had a Sunday off from the coffee shop.

"Just how hungry do you expect us to get?" Keisha asked as she watched me load up my bag. We were in my cottage, and I had prepared homemade pitas, falafel, and pickled vegetables. I was packing it up with some hummus, tahini sauce, and greens that we could assemble when we got there.

"Hungry! I plan to walk for ages and let the sun try to break through my SPF 50." I smiled at her. "Also, we're going to take some pictures for the blog. You can be my model," I said as I loaded two Nalgene water bottles in my bag. I also put in some thermoses of coffee and two adorable individual tiramisus I had made in mini mason jars. I had little lengths of twine tied around the jars with some sprigs of pine tied in.

We headed out, and I grabbed a little bag with four more dessert jars in it that I was going to take over to Benji and Max before we left. When I knocked on their door, Max opened it wearing jeans and a T-shirt, but his feet were bare. Why I found this sexy was beyond me, but it was. Very.

"Hi Lanie. Keisha. Headed somewhere?" He looked over my outfit of cutoff shorts and a loose shirt that showed the top of my swimsuit. I also had on a baseball cap, causing me to have to look up more than usual to meet his gaze.

"Beach day," I said as I pulled the desserts from my bag. Benji came running to the door and excitedly said, "I want to go to the beach. Dad, can we go to the beach too?"

"Not today, buddy. Sorry. We have to go to Grammie and Grampie's house to help them with their basement clear-out. But soon." He turned back to us. "It's a good day for it."

"I made some desserts and wanted to leave a few for you," I said, handing two of the little jars to Max and two to Benji. "They're mini tiramisus. Benji's are just the lady finger cookies with mascarpone cream. Yours have coffee, Max, so don't mix them up. Unless you want a caffeinated four-year-old."

Max laughed and asked Benji to take the jars to the kitchen as he relieved me of the bags I was carrying. "Let me load these in your car for you. Keisha, I can grab yours too," he said and raised his eyebrows in question.

"Mine are light," she said. "I'm good. Lanie's have all the food."

"Max, I'm fine. You don't have to do that," I tried to argue as he stepped out of the house and shut the door.

He loaded them in my car and opened my door for me. He placed his hand on the small of my back and guided me into the car. "Have a great day off," he said softly as I slid through the tight space between his body and the door.

"Watch your feet," I said, looking down at his still bare feet. "The rocks are sharp. You should have put on shoes."

He flicked the bill of my hat, then shut the door and waved to us as I started to back the car up.

"Girl," Keisha hissed as we took off. "That's some tension. Holy crap! I thought there was something going on, but I didn't know it was like that."

"Keisha, no!" A wave of embarrassment washed over me. Admitting to liking Max would sound like I thought I actually had a shot with him, which was embarrassing. I didn't want Keisha to think I was that deluded. "I mean, sure, I think he's great and attractive. Who wouldn't? But it's not like that."

"He practically undressed you with his eyes. It is like that."

"Really? You think he looked at me like that? Do you really think so?" I was uncomfortable with the conversation, but I really wanted to know if Keisha thought it was possible Max actually saw me that way. How was it I could never quite kill the hope even when I was trying?

"For sure. I've seen him hanging around talking to you. I've seen him watching you at lunch. But this was different. You should go for it."

"Yeah?" I scoffed. "Just like that? Just go after him, right?"

"Yes, put Benji in his room and make a move. Damn, I'll watch Benji some night if that'll help."

"I don't know, Keisha. Sometimes I think maybe he might be interested, but then mostly I really don't think that's possible. You should see what his wife looked like. And the age thing. I literally look like a child compared to her."

"I don't care what she looked like. You're beautiful. Girl-next-door beautiful. And he digs it. For real."

"I'm not so good with this stuff. I've only had one relationship. One person. And it wasn't actually a relationship, so …"

Keisha settled herself further into her seat. "Ooh. Lanie's juicy past! This day is gonna be fun! Tell me."

Did I want to share this with someone? Finally? Saying it out loud might be a relief, but it felt like a mistake even as I took a deep breath and said, "Well, basically, I was my best friend's brother's dirty little secret. That's pretty much the story. I was vulnerable and stupid and thought I was in love. He was manipulative and cruel and eventually made me hate him."

"This is Jessa's brother? That best friend – the one you lived with?"

I had told Keisha a little about my past. She knew the basics about my mom leaving and me living with Jessa's family.

"Right, Ethan. I was fifteen when I moved in. He's two years older. I was the classic dumb teenager. Ethan was – is – the guy everyone wants to date. He's gorgeous and a life-of-the-party kind of guy. He played every sport in high school, and he always had a girlfriend. He started teasing me – like flirting teasing – when I moved in, but only when no one else was around. I mean, he did it a little before, but it was all the time after I moved in."

It was like I wasn't even in the car with Keisha anymore. The memories were playing out in my head as I spoke them out loud.

"He convinced me – well, he convinced me of a lot of things. That he liked me. That we needed to keep things secret or his family would get upset and that was a terrible thing to do to them when they were letting me live with them. That he needed to keep having girlfriends and ignoring me at school so 'no one would suspect.' He even convinced me that it looked better if he was actually mean to me in front of his family and friends. He called me 'pixie stick' and 'baby' all the time – and not in the good way. Pixie stick because he said I was skinny and childish. And baby in the way like, 'Does the little baby need her pacifier? Is the little baby gonna cry?' after he tripped me in the hallway in front of all his friends. He also convinced me we secretly loved each other and that I should sneak into his room when Jessa fell asleep. He convinced me go to Planned Parenthood and start the pill. And he convinced me that, aside from pleasing him when I could manage it, I was pretty worthless."

Keisha had been quiet while I spilled my shame all over the car. She had listened patiently, but I was focusing again on the present and could tell she was upset.

"Don't feel sorry for me," I said to her. "I was stupid. It was my own fault."

"No," she said, patiently but clearly angry. "You know that wasn't your fault. Would you say the same thing to me if I told you a story like that? You know you wouldn't."

"Maybe," I said. I knew, in theory, it wasn't my fault. That Keisha was right, and if I heard anyone else tell me something similar about their past, I would never think it was their fault. But my shame about all of this was deep. I'd taken help from Jessa's family and snuck around and kept secrets. I'd loved Ethan and, because of that, let him do things to me that weren't okay. Every time I thought about him, I felt small and stupid and worthless.

"How long did this go on?" Keisha asked.

"Too long. The whole time he was home until he graduated high school, but then he would come home from college and pick things back up. He told me no one else would ever want to sleep with someone as mousy and boring as me, and I would look like an idiot if I tried to go out with anyone else. That I would just be a joke. He told me he was used to me, and that's the only reason he could stand to be with me. If anyone ever showed the slightest interest in me, he reminded me that they just felt sorry for me, or they were desperate and thought I was an easy fuck because of my mom. He basically made sure I waited around for him to come back from college for his breaks. When Jessa and I finally moved out, I tried to end things, but he kept me on a string for a few years even after that. Once he finished college, though, he moved away for good. I was pretty much done with guys at that point. He had gotten physical and even more controlling once I moved out of his parents' house, and I was relieved when he moved away. I eventually even changed my number because he would still send me texts I didn't want to see or read."

"He hit you? And forced you? Is that what you mean?" Keisha sounded like she pitied me. Great.

"No. Not really. He persuaded and insulted and cajoled until I gave in. And the physical stuff – it was just kind of being rough with me. Squeezing my arms until he left bruises or shoving me around. He did enough to scare me but nothing that anyone would really notice."

"You should report him."

I laughed. "For what? Convincing a stupid girl to be with him? Last I heard, the police weren't interested in that."

She let out a big sigh, and I felt bad about starting our day with my depressing past.

"I'm sorry I unloaded this on you. I shouldn't have shared all of it. Please don't feel sorry for me. Or be annoyed. I promise I won't complain all day. I've just never really had anyone to tell. I couldn't tell Jessa obviously. And there wasn't anyone else. I'm really fine. It's been a long time since it happened. I'm okay and, most importantly, I learned my lesson. Having no man in my life is better than having that man."

"He's a total ass, and it's lucky he lives far away. If I ever see him—"

"Okay, Keisha. Settle down now." I looked over at her angry face. It was strange to see how much she cared about what had happened to me. I wasn't about to tell her that Ethan had moved back home. "Thank you. Really. You're a good friend. And now, beach day begins! Help me find a parking space," I said, ready to change the subject.

Chapter 11

We're worried about you," Max said as he helped me bring the last of the serving dishes from the tables to the barn sink. It had been raining all day, and we had moved the tables into the barn for staff lunch. Everyone was relaxed since the rain meant a lighter day of work.

"Who is we? And who are we worried about?" I asked as I started filling the big sink with soapy water.

"We is Benji and me," he said. Benji stepped into the space and nodded vigorously. "And the person we're worried about is you."

"Me? What are you talking about? I'm fine. Great even!" I was mystified by Max's words. I could tell they were teasing a little – especially since Benji was involved, but I had no idea where this was headed.

"You work too much, Lanie," Benji piped up. "You're always cooking and cleaning and I know you get to relax when we play together—"

Max raised his eyebrows at me comically from behind Benji.

"But," Benji continued, "you keep going to the coffee shop almost every weekend, and you even had to work at night some this week."

It was true. I had been called in to do some evenings lately. There was a regular staffer who had worked through her high school years, and she was quitting to give herself a break before leaving for college.

"I'm fine," I repeated. "And who exactly has the grounds to accuse someone else of working too much, Max?" I looked at him pointedly. "Pot, meet kettle."

"She's right, Dad. But I don't get the tea kettle part. But, yeah, you work too much too."

"I don't hold down a separate job on nights and weekends," Max argued.

"No, you're just taking care of a child," I countered.

"Fine," Max put his hands up in surrender. "We both work too much … which is why Benji and I want to invite you over for dinner tonight. And we can all relax and not work together."

I swear my heart skipped a beat in that moment. "Dinner? With you and Benji?" I repeated.

"Yes!" Benji exclaimed. "We're gonna cook for you and then we'll play a game or watch a movie or something. Dad said we could!"

"Whatever you want to do, Lanie," Max said. "Just let us cook dinner and take care of you a little, okay?"

***

The butterflies were killing me. I had walked into Max Parker's house dozens of times by this point but never like this. Never as an invited guest. I'd put on a lavender spaghetti-strap sundress with a short white cardigan. I wasn't dressed up, but I didn't know if it would be weird for me to be in a dress (even a casual one) instead of my usual work clothes. I had also thought it might seem weird to go over for dinner in my work jeans. Whatever. I was here, and it was too late to change.

"Dad, Lady Lanie's here," Benji yelled as he opened the door for me. "And she's wearing a dress!"

"Hi Benji," I said, kneeling down to give him a hug. "I brought cookies," I told him and gave him a container of coconut chocolate pinwheels.

Max appeared at the entrance to the mud room, and we stared at each other for a second. He was looking me up and down – I had to admit it seemed to be appreciatively. And I was taking in his bare feet again and the kitchen towel he had draped over his shoulder.

"Dad, cookies!" Benji said, tugging on Max's arm.

"That's great, Benji. Why don't you take them into the kitchen for me? I'll be there in just a second to check on the fish. You can finish decorating the table how you wanted."

"Yeah, Lanie, I'm decorating the table just like you and me do together! But I'm doing it all by myself."

"I can't wait to see it, Benji."

Benji ran into the kitchen, and Max approached me. "You look amazing," he said as he bent down to kiss my cheek. "Jesus, and you smell good. I mean you always do, but I don't get to—"

"Dad, there's smoke!" Benji yelled from the kitchen.

"It's just steam, Benji. I'll be right there." Max laughed a little and led me to the living room. He ordered me to sit down and relax, and left me there only to return quickly with a glass of iced tea he handed to me. He slipped my shoes off, picked my feet up, and set them on the coffee table before sternly saying, "Don't you dare straighten or clean a thing while you're out here."

I listened to the chatter of Max and Benji as they worked together in the kitchen, and I tried to calm my nerves. Milo approached me and gave me a curious look, as if to say, *What are you doing here at this time of day?* I waved him over to me and stroked his head. He quickly ascertained I was settled in, and he hopped on the couch, draping his front paws and face over my lap. I felt nerves, guilt about sitting and relaxing, but also a deep sense of relaxation and well-being. I suddenly felt like I had never been this comfortable in my entire life. Max's deep couch was well-worn, and my body sank in nicely. My mind began to get a little fuzzy as the conversation from the kitchen turned into a comforting hum, and Milo's warm body soothed my nerves.

"Lanie?" I heard and realized, coming out of sleep, that it wasn't the first time my name had been called. I opened my eyes and saw Max sitting next to me. He was on the edge of the couch but sideways and leaning into me. His hand was stroking my shoulder. "Lanie, dinner is ready."

Benji hopped up on my other side where Milo was still sprawled out. "Come on, Lanie. Come see the table!"

Benji hopped down, and Milo followed him into the kitchen. Max picked up my hands and looked at them as he caressed them with his own. "Come on," he said. "You can nap some more after we eat." He stood and pulled me gently until I was standing, our bodies so close to each other between the couch and coffee table, I could feel him from his chest to his thighs. I was very aware of my breath and the fact I hadn't said anything since he woke me up. Again, I was afraid of messing up the moment. I wanted to just stand there pressed up against him forever. I laid my cheek into his chest, and he hugged me to him, his fingers running through my hair.

"Let's go get some food in you, yeah? Then you can rest some more." He gave me a little kiss on my head and led me into the kitchen.

***

Maybe I should leave, I found myself thinking. It had been a perfect evening. Max had made a lovely, simple meal of baked fish and roasted vegetables. Benji had proudly welcomed me to his kitchen table decorated with fresh flowers and a picture he had colored on top of each plate. We finished things off sitting in front of the TV watching *Dinosaur Train* with coffee and the cookies I had brought. Benji had gone back and forth between cuddling with me and jumping up to sing or dance or act something out from the cartoon.

It was getting late, and Max was upstairs putting Benji to bed. He had bathed him, and Benji had come down so we could read a story all together, but now Max was putting him down for the night. He had asked me to wait, but now I wondered what we were doing. Did he feel sorry for me? Did he think I was an easy and convenient option because I was here, crazy about him, and I'd be leaving soon? Was this something he did in the summers since his wife died? Or maybe I was the first, and this seemed like a good option now that his old housekeeper wasn't in the picture anymore?

I needed to protect myself, but maybe if I could pretend it was real – at least for a little while longer. Maybe I could deal with the heartbreak later? I mean, it's not as if there wouldn't be heartbreak when the summer was over – whether I enjoyed this moment or not. Maybe it was smart to pretend a little? My relationship with Ethan had left so much to be desired in every way – including our physical relationship. He was anything but giving. And, since Ethan, there had only been a couple of clumsy kisses with a few dates orchestrated by Jessa. Maybe this was something I should do – if that's where it was headed. And it seemed like it, right? If he could use me or pay attention to me because he felt sorry for me, couldn't I do the same? After all, he was also someone to feel sorry for. No, that wasn't right. Even as a widower, he would never be some pity hookup. But I did think he needed affection, and couldn't I take pleasure in being the one to give that to him even if it didn't mean anything more to him?

Or maybe I should just leave. I ended up back at square one and went through all the arguments for and against again.

I was starting on round three of this mental loop when I noticed Max looking at me from the bottom of the stairs. "He's out," he let me know. "I love him, and I'm grateful for his energy, but this moment is a highlight of my day."

He walked over to the couch and sat down next to me. He touched the edge my dress. "We need to talk, Lanie."

I don't know what I expected, but it wasn't that statement said with an accompanying sigh. "Talk?" I squeaked. "Is something wrong?"

"No," he said quickly. "Well, yes, but I've given up fighting that particular battle."

All I could hear was that he had said something was wrong. Was he still mad at me on some level? Did he mean he had tried to fight through the unattractiveness of my shortcomings like Ethan had? That since I was the one here (convenient, like I had been for Ethan), he had wanted to try to make it work? That he just couldn't get past how I was?

"What did I do? What battle do you mean?"

"Not you, sweet girl," he took my hand but continued facing straight ahead. "You didn't do anything wrong. It's me."

My mind was spinning. *Is this an "it's not you, it's me" thing? Why is he taking my hand if he's stopping things? What battle is wrong but given up on?*

"Look," he finally began. "I should never have kissed you that day. Damnit, I never should have even started looking at you. I tried not to for the longest time."

I thought back to the first week we met when he had avoided looking at me. He definitely had.

"You wouldn't even talk to me," I said. "You talked to Jessa about me and called me her little friend." It hurt my chest thinking about it. "Why did you do that? Why was it wrong?"

"So many reasons," he said, turning his head to look at me. "You're too young. You're too sweet. And now, even worse, you work for me. Those are reasons enough, but then I could add in that I'm a single dad with baggage who works too much. That pushes it way over the top."

I pulled my hand out of his hold. I couldn't argue that I was young. And, if by sweet, he meant inexperienced or naive, I probably was by his standards. My only experience was with Ethan, and he had been firmly in control of that

situation. I couldn't argue with his strikes against me, so
what did I have to say?

"I think I should probably get going now," I said,
starting to stand up.

"No, Lanie. Let me finish," he pulled me back down
and onto his lap. "I'm trying to say – I know I'm wrong here,
but I've already given up fighting it. Fighting the pull I feel
toward you. I kissed you and, if you'll let me, I know I'm
going to do it again. But I need you to really think about it.
You have to decide you want this between us. Especially
because you work here. Everything can go back to the way it
was anytime you want. No questions asked and no pressure
to change your mind. Okay?"

"Oh," I said, trying to decide if I should remain stiffly
perched on his thighs with my back ramrod straight or sink
into him, which is what I really wanted to do.

"So, if you'll allow it …" His finger traced the curve
under my knee and then he abruptly shook his head. "But not
right now," he said, forcing us both on our feet.

"What?" I shrieked as I found myself standing and
suddenly no longer perched on his sturdy lap. The right side
of his mouth quirked upward in the most adorable way.
"Well, when?" I asked, a little desperately. I think I
whimpered a little.

He chuckled and said, "We'll see. Not sure, but soon. When you're ready. Right now, we're going to grab a beer or some wine, and I get to find out more about you. I never get the chance to talk to you, Lanie." He pulled me to him. "What do you like to drink? Hm? Do you like beer, wine?" He stroked a lock of my hair and pushed it behind my ear. "Are you a hard liquor kind of girl who surprises everyone and drinks them under the table?" My eyes closed as I found myself leaning into his touch. "See," he continued, "I want to know these things."

We walked into the kitchen, and he pulled an IPA out of the fridge and looked at me with his eyebrows raised in question.

I shook my head no, and he closed the door. "So, what will it be then?" he asked.

"Oh, um, well. Nothing really. Or just some water. I don't like to drink."

"What – ever?" he asked, surprised. "I'm not planning on more than the one bottle if that's what you thought. I never have more than one when Benji's home."

"No, it's not that. And, yes, I guess to answer your question, I don't ever like to drink. My mom and then some other people … Let's just say they spoiled it for me. I don't like to be around it."

Max put his bottle back in the fridge and went to put water in the tea kettle. "Tea, then," he said. "We'll do some tea at the kitchen table. Very innocent and less likely to lead to the aforementioned kissing."

"Max," I laughed a little. "You don't have to do that. You can have your beer. I meant I don't like to be around it in a bigger way – not you just having a beer. It won't bother me."

"Would you admit it if it would?" he asked, looking me directly in the eyes. "I'm pretty sure you wouldn't."

I just shrugged because he was right.

"That's what I thought," he said and pulled out boxes of various teas and some mugs. Once we settled on our tea selections and had our steaming cups ready, we sat facing each other at his kitchen table. He was right. There was a bubble of intimacy, but it wasn't the kind that was going to have him kissing me anytime soon. It was the kind that had him asking me questions like where my love of cooking came from.

"Well, growing up, it was just my mom and me, and food was sometimes an issue …" I looked at him, embarrassed but trying to answer his question. I wanted to share myself with him, for better or worse, but I was really hoping he wouldn't just feel sorry for me. "I watched cooking shows on TV. They were relaxing, and sometimes … sometimes I was hungry." My cheeks burned as this truth stung. "My mom never held down a steady job, and she was more interested in ensuring she had other things. Food wasn't her priority. As I got old enough to think about actually making some of the food I saw, I began to understand that flour and butter were relatively cheap and stretched pretty far, so I got into baking. I could usually get enough money from my mom to buy a bag of flour and other basics like eggs and milk. Maybe not gallons of milk to go through boxes of cereal but a gallon to bake with. My mom had a sweet tooth, so that didn't hurt. Once I started baking, she would sometimes be interested in the result. When she finally took off for good with her man of the month, and I moved in with Jessa, I had to give it up. One thing we did have at Jessa's was regular meals. It was cereal for breakfast, school lunches, and Hamburger Helper for dinner, but it was consistent. And it wasn't really okay for me to be taking up space in their kitchen. I got to bake a little at work, but my boss is kind of funny about change. He has a few set recipes, and that's what we make. He has never been interested in doing anything new. So when we moved out into our own apartment, it was like everything opened up for me. I could bake anything I wanted and finally start to cook as well. I had to be careful since my habit could get expensive, but I learned what I could afford. Cooking here is like paradise. All the fresh vegetables and the stuff from the Dairy and Co-op … It's like I landed in my dream world."

Max kept asking me questions about my favorite bakes growing up and my favorite meal to cook for myself. "Smoked salmon quiche," I quickly informed him.

"You haven't made that one yet," he protested.

"I have!" I argued. "You asked what I made for myself. I've had it in the cottage a few times."

"Well, I want to try it," he said, seeming a little sulky that he hadn't gotten to yet.

"Fine," I giggled. "I'll make it for breakfast some morning. But I'm not sure how Benji will feel about it."

"Who's giving any to Benji?" he asked, his chocolate eyes twinkling at me.

"So," I said, "what about you and farming."

"Well—" he started.

"Wait!" I said. He looked surprised at my interruption but waited. "I have to tell you I already know about this a little."

"What do you mean?" he asked, confused.

"I mean … I'm not good at pretending, and I already listened to some gossip about you – not that she was being gossipy; she was being really nice – from Willow at the Co-op. I just want you to know because I can't sit here and pretend like I don't know something if I do. I'm sorry. But all I know is that you didn't grow up on a farm and you bought this place after you graduated from college. And that it was the farm Willow grew up on."

"Ah," he said. "Co-op gossip. I should have considered the things you would be picking up there or from my crew."

"But no one has told me about what you think or feel or like. That's what I really want to know – like what made you want to buy a farm?"

"What I think or feel or like? Hmm." Max told me all about growing up in a farming area and not being part of it. His dad was a math professor, and his mom was an elementary school teacher. They expected him to go into some kind of teaching too, but he was fascinated by the agriculture program when he went to college and the internships he did where he finally got to understand what life on the farms he grew up around was like. He also told me about how his mind would wander during his business classes to new things he could try in farming to make it more sustainable – both from a land stewardship perspective and as a sustainable business.

"But there's a bit of sustainability that I got unfairly and at too high a cost. And it's hard for me to accept the leg up I got as a new farmer," he concluded, and it was clear this piece of information really bothered him. "When Claudia died ... well, we had a life insurance policy. In the end, she hated how much I had to work to keep the farm going in those early years, and now I'm able to set up some programs and organize certain things that allow me more time with Benji only because that policy let me pay off the mortgage and set up a college fund. I think she would see that as the ultimate slap in the face. And I wouldn't blame her."

The silence hung in the air as we both thought about what he had shared.

He wouldn't look me in the eye after that, so I reached out and put my hand on his that was resting on the table. "You can't think that way, Max. She had to have loved you, despite the problems you had." I stroked his beautiful hand with my thumb. "Anyone who loved you would want to give you the gift of less worry and more time with Benji. I'm sure she would be happy for those things." I said it, but I still felt a prick of irritation that Max would think his wife would begrudge him this. What kind of cruel things had she said to him?

We talked beyond when it was wise to do so, given our early morning the next day. When we agreed we both needed to get some sleep, Max insisted on walking me to my cottage.

"But Benji …" I said as he ushered us out the side door, pushing Milo back in and telling him he needed to stay in the house.

"I have a monitor that goes to my phone. Sometimes I have to get up and check something in the night, so I got the monitor. And it's only a few steps away. Besides, knowing I need to get back to him will allow me to be a gentleman and not beg you to let me inside to say goodnight to you properly."

"Fine then," I blew out a small breath of feigned exasperation. "Walk me home if you must."

He did just that, and when he began to say good night after hugging me, I was the one who grasped the front of his shirt with both my hands to stop him. I was immediately embarrassed at being so forward and felt the blush creep over my face, but I really didn't want him to leave quite so soon.

"Sorry," I said. "Just…"

"What is it, Lanie?" He pulled me toward him by my hips, his hands burning through the thin fabric of my dress. I felt all of him up against me and I shuddered. "Did you want something?" he grinned confidently. "You can tell me what you want."

His cockiness irritated me just enough that I started to try to pull back. It was embarrassing enough that I physically stopped him from leaving, but I wasn't going to make it worse by begging for a kiss. He knew what I wanted, and his teasing was a little painful. It felt like he was laughing at me.

"No, sweetheart. Don't pull away. I'm sorry – I was just teasing. You're going to have to learn my teasing ways. Or, I guess I'll have to learn your teasing limits. Or maybe we'll meet somewhere in the middle. Come here, sweetheart. You know I want to kiss you – it's practically all I think about."

He stroked the hair along my hairline and pulled me even closer to him as he began to kiss along my jaw in a line to my lips. When he got there, he nibbled and sucked and bit in the softest, sweetest way until I opened to him – fully and completely. Instinctually, reflexively. His hands cradled my face, and he murmured and groaned each time he tried to pull himself away. I forgot we were outside the little cottage. I forgot to feel self-conscious. Thoughts pretty much stopped existing for me, and I just felt. I felt this amazing man wrapped around me, kissing me so tenderly and making it clear he wanted to keep kissing me. Which is why I was so startled when I felt his phone suddenly buzzing in his front pocket.

"Christ," he said, reluctantly forcing himself to pull away. "That's the motion detector for Benji's monitor. It's probably just Milo getting into his bed, but I should go check."

"Of course," I said, starting to come back to earth a bit. "Goodnight, Max. Thanks for dinner and for the company and for …"

"Good night, sweet girl. Get some sleep. I'll see you in the morning."

Chapter 12

The next few days I tried to avoid falling into that hazy place where all I could do was feel and hope. If my idea was to soak it up, enjoy it, and be prepared for the eventual heartbreak, I needed to mitigate the level of damage by not actually feeling all my feelings.

Max and I shared some lingering touches as we brushed against each other near the coffee pot in the mornings or we'd give each other knowing looks at the lunch table, but, other than that, we didn't really get a chance to spend any time alone together as we both went through the motions of our week. I had been hoping there might be some time we could spend together this weekend since I didn't have to work at the coffee shop on Sunday, but instead, I got to dread meeting his parents.

They only lived a few miles away, and they often visited one another on weekends, but, so far, I hadn't seen or met them. Max had already promised them that he and Benji would come for lunch, and he'd asked me to come as well. I really hadn't wanted to, but he said his mom had been wanting to meet me since she had heard so much about me from Benji.

"Meet me as Benji's nanny?" I had asked.

"Yes," Max had said. "But also as my … friend. Benji isn't the only one who has told them a lot about you." I didn't want to meet them as Max's "friend," but I knew it was only a matter of time before we would meet given the back-and-forth visits between the family, so I finally agreed when Benji also began asking if I would go.

David and Pam Parker were Max's educated parents who had clearly been supportive and wonderful given how Max had turned out, but I doubted they would think much of a parentless girl who'd only graduated high school and worked at a coffee shop.

"Grammie loves the chickens, Lanie," Benji informed me as we collected eggs from the coop. It was still one of my least favorite tasks on the farm. I liked watching the chickens, but I did not enjoy going into their space and, although I knew they weren't going to hurt me, I always got spooked anytime they moved or made a noise.

"Is that right?" I said, hurriedly collecting the last of the eggs and turning to leave the coop.

"Yes. She's not scared like you. She tries to pet them and talks to them when she takes their eggs. She would laugh if she saw you with them."

I knew things were bad when a four-year-old was hurting my feelings and making me feel even more on edge. This impending meeting was fraying my nerves.

Things didn't get easier as we parked in their driveway that Sunday afternoon. I was in the front of the cab with Max, but all he could do was pat my hand in reassurance since Benji was strapped onto his booster seat behind us.

Benji was jumping out of the truck before I could process the well-kept cape house in front of me. It was painted a sweet, pale yellow with crisp white trim and shutters.

I knew I wasn't going to have a horrifying moment of remembering Mrs. Parker as one of my early teachers because Max and I had already talked about her teaching in the school local to the farm, which was a smaller school than where I had gone in Beecham. But I also knew from the pictures in Max's house that the family resemblance was strong, so I felt I knew her a bit when she came rushing out to pick up Benji. She had Max's rich dark hair and eyes as well as his beautiful features. What she didn't have was his height. That all came from Mr. Parker. As he walked into the yard, it was clear he carried that height differently than Max, though. He had the air and cadence of an academic. I figured he had a pipe in his library that he enjoyed every night from the looks of him in his sweater vest and wire-rimmed glasses. Whereas Max and his mother radiated warmth, the coldness coming from his dad explained where Grumpy Max emanated from when he was not his usual self.

"Milo, sit!" Mr. Parker firmly commanded. Milo instantly listened and heeled by his side.

"Benji, peanut, I missed you!" Mrs. Parker said as she pulled him up on to her hip. He was a little guy but a bit big for his grandmother to tote him around. It was clear she still considered him her baby.

"Grammie, I taught Milo two new tricks this week. I want to show you. Well, Lady Lanie helped, but we got him to bring the ball back after we throw it, and we taught him to play dead! It's so funny!"

"Mom, Dad," Max said as he made his way around to my side of the truck. "This is Lanie."

"Hi, Lanie." Mr. Parker reached out and gave me a quick handshake.

"Lanie!" Mrs. Parker exclaimed as she reached out to hug me. "At last."

Strangely, Mrs. Parker's face did not match her words and actions. The warmth in her tone and her eyes disappeared as she turned her attention to me.

"Hello, Mr. and Mrs. Parker," I said, trying to make sure I spoke up. I tried to look at each of them as I talked but mostly kept moving my eyes to the top of Benji's head. "Thanks so much for ..." I hesitated. Inviting me? Had they invited me? Did they even really want me here? "Thanks so much for – for having me," I finished.

Max put his hand on my back and rubbed gently. "What's for lunch, Mom? I'm starving."

Mrs. Parker laughed as she led the way into the house. "You always are!"

***

First impressions are unreliable in this family. That's what I had decided as my offer to help clear the dishes after dessert was rejected. Mrs. Parker was not warm. She was an iceberg who knew how to freeze a person out far better than I did. She was a master. In my case, I never felt welcome anywhere and always assumed I was in the way, so she really didn't need to work so hard. I would have felt unwelcome even without her making it obvious. But she had made her point very clear: she did not want me developing any sort of relationship with her boys.

Any time Max tried to pull me into the conversation or, embarrassingly, into the spotlight by talking about how good I was with Benji or with a description of some of the food that I had made, Mrs. Parker made a dismissive remark like, "Yes, that's nice," or "Well, then." And then she would immediately bring up some conversation that was clearly intended to exclude me. She would talk about Uncle Joe or Mary Ellen at her work. She even talked warmly about Mrs. Harris, the former cleaner/cook/nanny – "Remember when Mrs. Harris cleared out the attic so well? The woman was a wonder."

Max was obviously uncomfortable and growing impatient with his mom's rudeness. And that's what it was. She was blatantly being rude to me, although she was wrapping it up in cold politeness, staking her ground and making it clear I wasn't welcome on it. I wasn't really bothered for myself. My expectations were exceedingly low about my ability to be accepted by Max's parents. But I was bothered for Max. I felt him tensing next to me and trying so hard to get his mom to like me.

Mr. Parker looked a little surprised at Mrs. Parker's iciness, but he kept his words to himself. Benji was thankfully oblivious. He remained his sweet self and chattered to his grandmother about the days we spent together – the walks we took, the food we made, and the games we played. He was my clueless cheerleader, and it was driving his grandmother crazy. She was visibly growing weary of the number of times she had to change the subject.

After refusing for the fifth time to let me help her with anything, she stood to clear the table. She removed the cookies I had brought from the far edge of the table where she had strategically placed them and the remains of the pie she had baked from the center. While she was in the kitchen, I turned to Max and asked if we could head back to the farm. I could tell he was determined to try to make things better, and I knew he wanted to stay in order to do that. But it wasn't going to happen, and he was just getting more and more frustrated.

"Max, maybe we should just head out for now. You and Benji could even come back if you wanted, but I think maybe I should get back."

Mr. Parker stood and took some dishes to the kitchen.

"Lanie, I don't get what's going on here. I think if we just—"

"Max, please. I'm okay, but I think it's time for me to go." I put my hand on his forearm and looked up at him.

He searched my face and considered for a tense few seconds before finally breathing out, "Okay, sweetheart. Let's go."

"Benji," he hollered into the kitchen where Benji had followed his grandparents. "Let's go, buddy. We need to get back to the farm. Go get Milo, would you?"

"But, Dad," Benji came running in, "we haven't even played Jenga yet with Grampie.

Mr. Parker followed Benji into the room and said, "Next time, peanut," in the gentlest voice ever. He turned to me and took my hand again and shook it gently, this time wrapping his other hand around our joined hands. "Thank you, Lanie, for all you're doing for him. You're obviously doing a great job. We appreciate it."

He gave Max a significant look that made it clear he supported us leaving, and he gave me another look that seemed to indicate he was apologizing for how things had gone at lunch.

"Yeah, Dad, all right," Max said. Then he looked down at me and said he would meet me at the truck. As I was putting my shoes on by the front door, I could hear his voice as it rose in the kitchen with his mother. He was really unhappy, and I hated that I was causing this friction. I was obviously the problem, and I just wanted the day to be over.

"Thanks, Mr. Parker," I mumbled as I slipped out the door.

***

The ride home was quick and filled with Benji's stories and questions. When we pulled up to Max's house, he asked me to come in for some coffee. He set up an excited Benji in the living room and told him he could watch an episode of *Dinosaur Train* before they needed to go out for evening chores, and he escorted me into the kitchen where he started making coffee.

It was hard to watch him. He was angry but also filled with frustration. He was closing cabinets a bit too harshly and banging cups on the counter. He kept looking over at me, trying to assess if I was okay. Other than being bothered by how he was feeling, I really was fine. He didn't seem to understand that this was what I expected; it was par for the course for me. I was okay with myself. I really was, but I had no expectation that his mother would like me. My own mother didn't care much for me. Why should his? I felt bad that I couldn't be different for him – that I couldn't be someone his mom could like. But I wasn't surprised by it.

I wanted to reassure him and make him feel better, so I tried several topics like asking him about Becca, the chicken who kept stealing eggs from other chickens and rolling them into her own nest. Or telling him some of the gossip I had overheard about the possibility of a love triangle between Cassandra, Spruce, and Micah, which was causing friction between Cassandra and Spruce and leaving Scott out in the cold. I tried to bring as much energy and cheer as I could to the conversation because Max was only grunting.

He sat as he slid coffees in front of each of us at the little kitchen table. Then he scraped his hand through his hair and sighed, taking my hand in his. He took several deep breaths as he focused on where he was stroking my hand and finally said, "Sweetheart, I'm so sorry. I don't understand what just happened. I've never seen my mom like that."

He was in agony, and that was squeezing my heart. I knew this wasn't permanent, but he really cared how I felt and that was something new and special and so dear. I reached up to stroke his hand with my free one. "I'm fine. Everything was fine. Your mom wanted to focus on you and Benji, and that's how it should be. Please don't worry about me. Or about anything. She has no reason to want me around. This was her time with you and Benji. I get it. It's totally fine." I so badly wanted to reach over and rub away the furrow between his brows, but it felt like an overstep, an invasion of his space.

"Damnit, Lanie, it's not fine. It makes no sense. I'm going to talk to her again. Nothing about that was okay." He looked so incredibly distressed, and his hand started squeezing mine a little too tightly as he distractedly looked out the window next to us. He continued saying things like how he needed to talk to his dad to understand what the hell was happening, and how he was going to have a hard time forgiving his mom. Feeling this way about her was clearly overwhelming him as he had not expected anything to go down at lunch the way it had.

I couldn't help myself any longer. I reached across the table and stroked his cheek, then rubbed gently at the line between his brows. "Max, stop worrying, please. I'm so fine. There's no reason she needs to like me. I don't need to go again and upset your time with her. I am okay. Really. You need to let this go. She's probably hoping for you to get more serious with Angela or someone like Willow – or any other woman."

He grabbed my arms and guided me out of my chair and onto his lap. "Any other woman? What exactly are you talking about, Lanie? Who the hell is Willow and how do you know Angela? And, if you know Angela ... Again, what the hell are you talking about?"

My face flamed as I answered because I really didn't want to have to have a conversation about this. "Well, I meant Willow from the Co-op. She seems like someone who would be a good match for you, and she talked about you, and it seemed like maybe she liked you. And Angela – well, I don't know her, but Benji mentioned she was your friend and would be at your parents a while ago when you went for dinner and how funny she was and ... Well, I know there are lots of women who would want your attention, and I'm sure your mom is hoping you'll settle down with one of them. That's all. It's totally understandable. I would want that for you. You deserve to be happy."

"You would want that for me?" he asked with an eyebrow raised. "You want me to settle down with Willow, an acquaintance of mine, or Angela, a seventy-year-old retired sustainable agriculture professor who I like to socialize with to pick her brain? That's what you would like to see me do?"

I was starting to feel pretty stupid sitting on his lap while he revealed more about the women I had imagined were taking up what little free time he had that wasn't spent with me. He said all this with a twinkle in his eye and had been rocking me back and forth on his lap. He was teasing me now, and I didn't want to feel stupid for what I had imagined. It was totally reasonable to assume he was still talking to, spending time with, or even dating other women.

Even though it was reasonable, it didn't mean it felt good to think about or talk about, and his teasing wasn't helping, so I found myself trying to escape his arms and his lap. But as I squirmed to try to get up, he squeezed me tighter and brought me closer to him, pressing me to his chest.

"Lanie, sweetheart, I'm not interested in anyone else. Did you really think I would do this with you and someone else at the same time?" He dropped kisses on the top of my head and stroked up and down my arm.

I absolutely did think he would "do this" with me and someone else at the same time. In my experience, that wasn't unusual, and I knew this wasn't headed somewhere serious. I wasn't an idiot. I wasn't a girl someone like Max would ever commit to. And that was okay. He really should be with someone like Willow. Someone beautiful and smart and respected in his world. I just didn't want to think about it, and I especially didn't want to talk to him about it.

"Max, it's fine. I don't want to talk about this, okay? Whether it's Angela or Willow or whoever, I get what your mom would want for you and that's okay. Please, can we just drop it?"

He searched my face and then dotted kisses all over it before finally reaching my mouth. In between soft kisses, he said those lovely things that melted my heart like "sweet, sweet girl" and "why would I want anyone else" and "I want you to care" and "Jesus, you're killing me." Finally, he pulled back and sort of set me away, encouraging me to go back to my seat and drink my coffee. "Benji ..." he said as he took a deep breath.

His kisses and touches and words were like a drug to me, and I was still woozy as I took my seat and sipped my coffee. Hearing the ending song from Benji's show in the living room, Max picked up the topic of Becca, the chicken, again. We kept that up, pulling Benji into the conversation as he came into the kitchen, until Max took Benji out for some farm chores, and I went back to my cottage to do some planning and prep for the week ahead.

Chapter 13

As August was approaching, I knew things were going to be more rather than less busy on the farm. I was starting with Benji just after six each morning. The farm work wasn't finishing until after six each night, but I was scheduled every night for the next week at the coffee shop because they still hadn't replaced the girl who had recently quit. Max was having to keep Benji occupied while he tried to finish things up every evening so I could leave for work. He was exhausted. But he also kept apologizing that I was having to work so much and kept trying to give me breaks throughout the day. The truth was that spending my days taking care of things around the house, playing with Benji, and preparing the farm lunch – yeah, it was work, but I loved it. I could definitely have done without the late shift at the coffee shop, but the rest of it? I loved it all. And if Max had a minute to spare to give me relief? Well, I wanted to spend that minute with him anyway, so usually it meant walking with Benji and Milo and catching up on our days in those few moments or simply being able to see each other while playing tag or hide and seek all together.

Every time I looked at the calendar and started the mental countdown of my days left with Max and Benji, I wanted to bring back up every wall I possessed to protect myself. Then I would remind myself that I could have four more weeks of bliss and affection and kindness and care followed by the impending heartbreak. Or I could put up my walls and just have heartbreak without any of the good parts. It wasn't hard to convince myself to keep pretending for a while. The hard part was that the pretending kept leading to hope, and that was something I knew I needed to kill. It was vital to always remember it was pretend because if I believed it was real, the result when it ended would be far worse than heartbreak.

I slid into bed Friday night after my late shift mulling over all of this. I was looking forward to the following day. Max would only do the essentials around the farm, as he really did try to take most of the weekend off. His crew who did some harvesting, cleaning and prepping veggies, and made CSA deliveries would come in and that would take up a bit of his time, but, other than that, he had already told me how much he was looking forward to spending time together over the weekend. I had a morning shift at the coffee shop on Sunday, but I had Saturday off. I was going to sleep in and then look forward to seeing Max and Benji.

I dozed off and was dreaming about playing hide and seek with Benji in his house. I was going into every room, looking everywhere, but it was all empty. In fact, the house was mostly bare, and some of the furniture that was left was covered in sheets. I was frantically trying to find Benji when I realized my phone was ringing, and I fully woke up.

A late night/early morning phone call wasn't completely unusual for me. I instantly knew it would be Jessa calling, and it was. "Jessa, what's wrong?" I answered.

She was crying and couldn't get coherent words out. I realized I needed to get out of bed and start getting dressed. "Jessa," I interrupted, trying to sound stern enough to get her to be clear. "What is happening? Are you okay? Do you need a ride? Are you hurt?"

"Jet," she said between sobs.

"Oh, Jess. What about Jet? Did he do something?" I was going to kill him if he'd touched her.

"He left!" she wailed. "He left, and I don't know what to do. How could he leave me? We were perfect together."

I had lived through a lot of Jessa's breakups. She went through men like a runner went through water. She was a dramatic person, but she liked to be in control. Her reaction to a breakup was usually anger with a side of a desire for revenge. This typically involved getting dressed up and going to a bar to find someone new to shove it in the old guy's face. But this devastation was completely unlike her. I couldn't understand why she liked Jet as much as she did, but it was clear she really did.

"Jessa, honey, it's okay. You're going to be okay. Did he do anything to you? Did he give you a reason?"

"No! No reason. He couldn't have meant it. He must've been feeling neglected or something. This can't be right. You know what? I'm gonna fix this. I'm getting dressed up and going down to his bar to confront him."

"Jess, no," I said as I pulled on my jeans and mentally checked through the things I needed to grab on my way out. Keys, wallet, phone – which would probably still need to be connected to Jessa while I drove to see her. "No, Jess, you need to sleep and consider things fresh in the morning. You don't want to go confront him at work. That's not going to solve anything tonight."

I needed to text Max to let him know I was leaving, but I couldn't decide if I should do it before or after I got to Jessa's. He wasn't going to be happy. We mostly avoided the topic of my best friend, but he thought she took advantage of me and that I shouldn't be friends with her. I couldn't get him to understand how much she had done for me growing up. He thought I was giving her too much credit, and he got angry when I talked about life with her family. He didn't like them much at all. Thank God he didn't know more about Ethan.

I didn't want him to get the message before I left and try to stop me, but I also didn't want him to worry if he heard my car and didn't know where I was going at midnight. Ultimately, I decided to send a simple text from my car just before pulling out of the driveway.

Hi Max – Jessa needs my help. She's at our old apartment and is really upset. I'm headed there now to help. Nothing to worry about. She just needs my support. I'll let you know when I'll be back tomorrow. xoxo, Lanie.

I had never typed "xoxo" in my life. I debated and worried over whether to add it, but I wanted him to know I wanted to hug and kiss him. He deserved to know that, right? So I hit send and drove away.

***

"He did what?" I shrieked.

Jessa and I had been on her couch for an hour. She was drinking vodka, although I was pushing the option of hot tea or coffee frequently. So far, I had learned that the breakup had happened about an hour before she'd called me, and it sounded final. The apartment was a mess. There were piles of dishes in the sink, old food containers scattered throughout, and dirty clothes and mail on the floor and on top of various surfaces. I learned that Jet had called her some pretty terrible names like a "clinging cunt" and a "dirty whore," and I also had just learned that he stole her rent money. She had given it to him and asked him to drop it off with the landlord the day before. That had precipitated the discussion that led to the breakup. When Jessa got home from work, the landlord stopped her to ask if she had the rent money. She said that Jet had dropped it off yesterday. When the landlord said he hadn't, Jessa went inside to ask Jet about it.

Jet had told her she was uptight and selfish, and he had needed the money for "things" and she needed to chill. The conversation had escalated from there, and it was clear to Jessa he no longer had any of the money she had given him.

"He stole money from you, called you horrible, filthy things, and you still want him back? Jessa, come on! What do you see in this guy? You have to let him go," I tried to reason with her for the hundredth time.

"No, I overreacted. He's a free spirit, and I know better than to put him in a box. I love him so much. I was just stupid to confront him about this." She collapsed into another round of sobbing.

I wasn't getting anywhere with her in the state she was in, so I shifted my attention to trying to get her to drink some water and rest. Dealing with her in this state was much harder than dealing with Benji even when he was tired and hungry.

Thinking of Benji reminded me to check my phone, and I saw two missed calls and three text messages from Max.

12:03am: *Are you all right? Call me.*

12:30am: *Lanie? Please be careful.*

12:45am: *Lanie? Are you okay?*

I quickly texted Max back to let him know I was fine, and that Jessa was upset because Jet had broken up with her. I told him she was drunk, and I was just trying to get her settled so she could get some sleep.

12:57am: *She's a big girl, Lanie. This isn't your problem.*

12:58am: *She's my friend, Max. I'm okay. I'll be home tomorrow.*

I regretted the message as soon as I hit send. *Home.* I'll be *home* tomorrow. How embarrassing to call his house my home. I hoped he understood I didn't mean it like that. Of course that wasn't my home; it was his home. I was the girl without a real home. That was what I had always been, and I was again mad at myself for these mental slips I was having – forgetting my place in this world. How things always turned out. Stupid to forget.

1:03am: *Okay, sweetheart. I just worry about you. Please get some sleep yourself and don't spend all your energy taking care of her. Come home and let me do that for you.*

That was a temptation. Max taking care of me was the best. Taking care of Max was also the best. Trying to let those comforting thoughts hum around in my mind while going through the motions of supporting Jessa, I finally was able to get a few hours of sleep as the sun began to rise.

***

"Jessa!" a voice yelled followed by pounding on her door. "Jessa, open the fucking door." I knew that voice. Fear made my heart rate skyrocket, and I broke into a sweat.

Ethan.

I was on the couch, and I found myself sitting up quickly and cowering toward the end farthest from the door. I had gotten Jessa into her bed a few hours ago. My old room was filled with Jet's garbage – guitars, clothes, and gaming stations. My mind was racing with my limited options as Ethan continued to pound on the door.

I jumped off the couch, grabbed my bag, and raced into Jessa's room. "Jessa!" I whisper-shouted. "Jessa, get up!" I patted her cheeks and pulled at her blankets. I could not do this. I couldn't be the one to deal with Ethan. "Jessa, please. Please wake up. Ethan's here and I can't …" What could I even say to her? Even if she was awake and sober. She thought I had an undying, unrequited crush on her big brother. She had no patience for it and had spent the time when Ethan was "with" me telling me he would never want me, and I needed to let it go. Even if she woke up to handle the situation, it would just mean both she and Ethan would treat me as they always had when they were together, which wasn't good. It was an area of my life where Jessa had never had my back. She never stuck up for me when Ethan tormented me. When he'd knocked me down at school and laughed at me, she'd laughed along. When he'd made fun of me at home, the whole family had enjoyed the show. Jessa was the spoiled brat of the family, but Ethan was the crowned prince. The golden child.

Jessa was not going to get up.

I had two choices – try to pretend no one was home and not answer the door, or answer it myself and see Ethan for the first time in four years. I wanted to not answer, but I knew there would be a price to pay later. Ethan would ask Jessa why she hadn't answered, and she would tell him I had been here and then when I finally did see him …

This is irrational, I said to myself. *He can't hurt you any longer. You are not a teenager living in his parents' house. You no longer think you are in love with him. You no longer think he is a good person. He's a bad person. You know this, so what are you afraid of?*

I steeled myself and stood to go answer the door. As I unlocked and opened the door, Ethan started saying, "Jesus, took you long enough, Jes—" He stopped when he saw me and grinned a little. "Lamie? Little Lamie Billings?" He stepped through the door. "Oh my God, it is you!" He grabbed me before I could step back, and hugged me, picking me up off my feet and swinging me a bit. "Where have you been hiding?" Then he quickly put me down and looked around. "Shit, where's Jessa?" he asked more quietly, making sure she hadn't been there to witness him hugging me.

I stood frozen in my spot, hoping we could make this quick. "She's asleep. Was she expecting you today?"

"Asleep? That's good. What's going on with you? I'm so fucking pissed at you for not answering me these last few years. What the hell is up with that? Look at you, you little pixie stick. Haven't grown a bit, have you? Come here. Let me see you. I missed you!"

He reached out to try to pull me toward him, but I backed away and walked to the other side of the room, putting the couch between us.

"So, it's like that, is it?" he asked, with a small sneer.

"Um, how are you, Ethan?" I tried to ignore where he was headed. "How have you been?"

"Well, pixie stick, I've been just fine as you can see," he said, pushing the blanket over and making himself comfortable on the couch. He patted the space next to him and put his feet on the coffee table, but I remained where I was. "I'm kicking ass at work and loving life. I told fucking Jessa that I wanted to fucking see you, but she's useless. Had to make this shit happen myself. I missed you, pixie. Come give me some love."

"Ethan, I'm sorry. I've been really busy. Actually, I need to go now. Work. I've got to get to work. I'm sure I'll see you around some time. Maybe you could stay until Jessa wakes up? She broke up with her boyfriend last night and had a little too much to drink." I headed to Jessa's room so I could grab my bag and leave, but Ethan continued talking as I walked back into the living room.

"You look good, pixie. Really. Come on. I've missed you. Come over here and let me remind you what you've been missing too." He reached out toward me as I headed for the door.

I tried to get there quickly, but he was on the side of the couch closest to it, and he jumped up and beat me there, blocking my way out. As he leaned against the door, he assessed me and said, "Think you're too good for me now, Lamie? Is that what you think?"

"No, Ethan. I just need to go. Please, can you just let me go?"

"Stupid little pixie. Some things just don't change right? Look at this place. You live like a pig. Just because you come from trash doesn't mean you have to live like that, you know? Have some self-respect."

I looked Ethan in the face for the first time in over four years. There were so many feelings swirling through me. Hatred, for sure. I was so mad at myself for ever thinking I loved him. For ever thinking he was worthy of love. That was really the key point. He wasn't worthy of my love. I also felt sorry for him. Sorry that he learned from his dad and had achieved success approaching life that way. Sadly, I still felt fear. Ethan was a volatile guy, and right now I was not giving him what he wanted. I had memories of what he was capable of even when I was giving him what he wanted, and it wasn't pretty. Lastly, I was so angry that he still had the power to make me feel bad about myself. This wasn't even my mess, but I still felt like he was right – that I came from trash, and I was trash.

"Lanie, come here," he tried again. He was using his coaxing voice – he had been so successful with it when I was a teenager. Why would it fail now? My skin crawled as he reached for me, and my heart rate spiked. When he wrapped his fingers around my forearm and tugged me toward him, I felt my stomach turn.

"Ethan, what are you doing?"

Ethan's smile dropped from his face as he looked over my shoulder at his sister. I could see him calculating his next move. "Just saying hi to Lamie here and keeping her from leaving," he said as he shoved me slightly away from him. "She was trying to leave the apartment with you drunk and asleep and without cleaning up her mess. I was trying to help you out, little sister."

He moved away from the door, and I didn't hesitate. I headed out the door immediately with a "Call me later, Jessa. Get some rest."

I could hear Ethan say, "Still a loser," as I ran from the apartment to my car and drove away as if he were chasing me.

Chapter 14

I drove for hours trying to calm my frenzied feelings, but I was running on little sleep and needed my bed. *Stupid, stupid – not* your *bed. You don't have a bed. You don't have anything just like your trashy mom didn't have anything. Because you're stupid and not worth anything better.* I kept catching my own eye in the rearview mirror and seeing Ethan's little pixie stick – the stupid girl no one wanted but he was willing to tolerate. The skinny, ugly girl who made people uncomfortable with her trashy mom and her inability to talk to anyone. The parasite who got by only by mooching off other people. That's the girl I kept seeing in the mirror as I drove.

I didn't want to see Max or Benji. I just wanted to get to the cottage and sleep without seeing anyone. Or without them seeing me. Of course, things rarely go the way you want, and Max was out the door almost immediately when I parked in front of his house. He came to meet me as I walked toward the cottage, and he tried to give me a hug right there on the path where anyone could see. I felt myself stiffen in his arms.

"Lanie, sweetheart, are you okay? I was worried about you." He ran his hands up and down my arms. "You look so tired,. Let's get you inside."

He tried steering me toward his house, but I stopped and turned toward the cottage. "I'm sorry," I said to him as I tried to pull away from the arm he had around me. "My phone died, and I didn't take my charger last night when I left. I am really tired. I didn't get much sleep last night, and I really just want to go to the cottage to crash." I looked up at him for the briefest of seconds before directing my gaze – no, my entire face to the ground. I didn't want him looking at my ugly, tired face anymore.

"Yeah, of course. Okay. Yeah, get some sleep this afternoon. What about tonight? Do you want to come over for dinner? I'll cook and Benji will decorate." He smiled at the thought.

"No. No, Max." I felt him tense next to me and fully remove his arm. "I'm sorry," I said looking at my feet. "I'm just really tired and not up for anything today. I'm sorry."

He put his hand to my cheek and angled my face up, so I had no choice but to look at him. Two heavy tears broke free and slid down my face. He stroked one away with his hand.

"Lanie, what is it? What's wrong? Did Jessa do something to you? Please talk to me."

I couldn't tell him about Ethan. There was way too much to tell. And I couldn't tell him I felt like a stupid, worthless person who just wanted to hide herself away from everyone. He would be so angry, but he also might realize that's who I really was.

So, I didn't say anything. But this time, when he pulled me into him, I hugged him back and let him hold me for a bit before I broke away and went into the cottage.

***

The next morning, I looked at my puffy eyes in the mirror while I got ready for my shift at the coffee shop. I had slept for hours, but fitfully. I would sleep and then wake up and cry, and then repeat over and over. I was thinking of the person I had been with Ethan and wondering if I was really any different now. I was still a person who commanded very little respect – I was easy for people to ignore or dismiss. The truth was, I encouraged people to ignore me and tried to go unnoticed most of the time. I was working the same job I had in high school and now had this job – the other job I did in high school, taking care of little kids. Ethan would have

things to say about that. He would think I was still doing the
work of a twelve-year-old. I wasn't progressing. I was still
the same girl I had always been. And no one ever had any use
for that girl.

But Max seemed to for some reason. And Benji. And
Keisha, and some of the others. They really did. Even though
I knew things with Max were temporary, I did believe he
cared. I didn't want to be that same girl, and I didn't want to
push these new people in my life away. But I was afraid I
was going to. Especially Max. Especially after yesterday. I
cringed, remembering.

I grabbed my phone, which was now fully charged,
and scanned the messages he had sent.

8:15am: *I know it's important to you – is Jessa okay?
Please call.*

5:00pm: *I'm glad you're still sleeping, but I hope I
get to see you tonight. I'm worried about you. What
happened?*

6:00pm: *If you wake up and want to come over,
please do. Benji and I are here, and we have dinner ready.
We'd love to see you.*

9:00pm: *Okay, so I hope you're still resting instead of
avoiding me. Benji is going to my parents tomorrow and is*

spending the night there. *I want to take you out tomorrow night. Please don't say no.*

10:00pm: *Good night, sweet girl.*

Mixed in with Max's texts were texts from Jessa as well.

10:00am: *What the hell, Lanie? Why did you tear out of here like that? Ethan thinks you're so weird and I have no idea what to tell him because that was really weird. What the hell?*

2:00pm: *So, I'm thinking maybe you could give me your half of the rent this month since Jet moved out. That way I could save the room for you for when you come back next month.*

2:01pm: *Also, I need to borrow my half of the rent since Jet took my money. I know it should be okay since I got you that other job. Let me know when I can get it. I have to pay the landlord Monday.*

I scanned the texts several times and thought about the differences between how Ethan and Max spoke to me. It never mattered how hard I tried to please Ethan, he always told me I was stupid and belittled me every chance he got. Max, on the other hand, was always full of praise for me. He always told me how impressed he was with the work I was doing on the farm and with Benji. He told me he was amazed at how I had thrived after what I had gone through growing up. I didn't see myself as thriving, but Max did. At least he never missed an opportunity to tell me. He made me feel good and capable and a little stronger.

I thought about whose voice had really been in my head for the last twenty-four hours and had to admit it was Ethan's rather than my own. It was usually someone else's voice in my head – my mom's, Ethan's, Jessa's. Those voices were not nice to me. And, I now realized, it was crazy for me to keep allowing them to be the voice in my head.

I picked up my phone and sent a text back to Max before heading out to work.

7:30am: *I'm really sorry about yesterday. I got lots of rest and feel better this morning. I have to go to work but would love to spend tonight with you. xoxo.*

***

The lavender dress again. I was sitting at my little table in the cottage, freshly showered, hair with a soft curl added and full makeup applied, which for me meant mascara and Chapstick.

But I was in the lavender dress. I didn't have much else appropriate for an actual date with Max. And I remembered how he had looked at me and touched me when

I wore it before. I wanted that again, but an actual date was so scary. Especially after yesterday. I knew Max was patient with me, but he couldn't possibly even guess at why I was the way I was. I thought it was likely his patience was going to wear thin soon, so I kept giving myself a pep talk. I wanted to greet him so enthusiastically and confidently that he would let yesterday go without too many questions.

I heard Benji's grandparents pull in to pick him up. I felt bad that I hadn't seen him since Friday. We had planned on spending time all together this weekend, and he was excited about it. If I weren't so nervous, if Max's mom didn't hate me, if I weren't in the lavender dress – I would have gone outside to give him a hug and tell him to have a good time. If, if, if.

When the voices died down, the car doors slammed, and I could hear the car driving away, I could practically feel every footstep Max took toward the cottage. I was breathing quickly. My heart was in my throat, but I got up to open the door for him.

Max stood on the little porch also looking nervous. He was wearing khaki pants and a light green untucked, button-up linen shirt. His short hair was carefully in place, and he was clean shaven. He didn't need to take any pains or dress up to look amazing. He always looked amazing, but it made my heart swell that he had done this … for me.

He was looking for the right words to say to me because he started and stopped more than once. He was afraid to spook me. Oh, the number I had done on him with my self-loathing. I wanted to grab him and hug and kiss him. Tell him I was sorry again, but all that emotion manifested only in me reaching out my hand and barely touching the fabric near one of the buttons on his shirt. I rubbed the fabric between my fingers, trying to make some sort of connection, but it told him enough.

He cupped my cheek and reached down to drop a soft kiss to my lips. "You look beautiful, Lanie. You always look so beautiful."

I kissed him back and, before long, got enough confidence to raise my hands up and around his neck. He picked me up a bit and hugged me tightly. "Are you ready for some fun tonight?" he asked, nuzzling my neck.

"I'm going to spend time with you, so, yes, I'm ready to have fun," I said smiling up at him.

Dinner and a beach walk. That was our date. Max drove me to a seafood place that had outdoor seating overlooking the water, and he mostly succeeded in forcing me to feel comfortable. He had encouraged me to grab a warm sweater before we left, and I brought it with me to the table. He talked to me about the menu instead of sitting in awkward silence while we both looked it over. He quickly rejected the wine and beer menus when they were offered and ordered waters for us both. He had gotten us a small table in the corner. While some people might have felt handled and stuck in a corner, Max knew what I needed. I felt taken care of, and I felt like I was in a protected, private corner where I could focus only on Max and not worry about everyone around us.

"How do you know what I need?" I asked after the server dropped off the appetizers.

He put a mini crab cake and two lobster spring rolls on my small plate before adding some to his own. "I'd love to read your mind, Lanie, but what do you mean? What are we talking about – what you need?"

"Just everything," I said as I looked at my food, itching to take a picture. "I feel more comfortable at this restaurant being outside than I would in some fancy dining room. I feel more comfortable tucked over here in the corner. It makes me uncomfortable to navigate this kind of stuff, but you are effortlessly doing it for me. How do you know?"

"Well," he said, reaching for his fork, "I pay attention. It's like … Lanie TV. I enjoy watching you. Seeing what brings a smile to you face. Seeing what makes you grimace. I mean, I don't like watching you uncomfortable enough to grimace, but I like watching to see if there's anything I can do to fix it. You deserve that. You deserve someone to take care of you. To look out for you. To make you smile."

"You don't have to do that. I mean, thank you, but you do so much even without all the extra. I just—"

"Lanie, it makes me happy. It really makes me happy. I'm glad it doesn't bother you – I worried about that at first."

"What do you mean? What did you worry about?"

"Just you're so young and innocent …"

"I'm not as innocent as you seem to think I am," I said, not loving that I was giving him some indication about my past with someone else.

"Well, that's a conversation we should maybe have later tonight," he said. "But you are still young and innocent. Vulnerable to the hardness of the world, even though you survive it on your own so admirably. And I was this asshole older dad just creeping on you."

"Max! You're not … that!"

"Yes, I definitely was. Am. I am an asshole for even noticing how beautiful you are. I didn't want to talk to you because I didn't want any more proof of how giving and kind you were. I didn't want to watch you pushing past your shyness to defend your worthless friend when I first met you. I didn't want to see when you had your guard down and smiled with Benji or Milo. God, that time I came the house to get something I'd forgotten and saw you and Benji being silly and dancing around the kitchen ... I just wanted to not notice any of it ... But I did. I couldn't help it. I noticed all of it. And then I got madder at myself for noticing. And I took that out on you after I knew Rich wanted to get to know you. I was trying to stay away from you, but there was no chance I was going to watch ... that happen."

I laughed and Max looked at me, confused. "Why is that so funny?"

"You're talking as if – I don't know. I'm still finding this hard to believe. That you would feel that way or that you would think Rich would. Just any of it. I know you heard my argument with Jessa that day. And I know you felt sorry for me after. Maybe you're feeling some protective thing, but you shouldn't. I can take care of myself. I don't want you to feel all conflicted because of that."

"No. That's not it. I don't feel sorry for you. I mean, it breaks my heart what you've gone through and wish I could make it go away, but I don't feel sorry for you. Despite everything being stacked against you, you can take care of yourself. But it makes me furious that you have to. And I do feel protective. Ridiculously so. That's what I mean. I want to take care of you. I *have* to take care of you. With the age difference, I was afraid that was a pretty creepy thing to bring to the table. I know you don't need a parent—"

"Max, it's a nine-year difference, not twenty-nine!"

"It doesn't matter. I know you don't need a parent, and I definitely don't feel parental toward you. But the protective thing. That's there. And the fact that you didn't really have someone to parent you and you did it yourself? That has been a lot of my conflict. I didn't know whether you would push back if you didn't like something. I saw you let Jessa – I'm sorry to say – take advantage of you—"

"She doesn't—"

"Hold on." He held up his hand to stop my interruption. "I saw you let her take advantage of you, and I saw how much capacity you had for love, and I was afraid if anything happened between us … the power dynamics – I would push you too much to let me take care of you. Even if you didn't want it. But I also saw you stand up for yourself in small ways over and over. Even with Jessa. You do let her take advantage of you. I'm sorry, sweetheart, but you do. But I can also see it's a choice. You choose when and what to allow. You have boundaries. You have self-preservation.

Thank God. I was relieved and so fascinated. I've never met anyone like you."

I looked down at my hands and squeezed my eyes shut for a few beats. This sounded serious. He sounded like he really cared for me. I mean, I knew he cared for me, but this didn't sound like it was a summer fling. He sounded like he had been considering this seriously from the beginning. I didn't know what to say, but I needed to process a little. I needed time to absorb what he was saying and what it meant, and that wasn't going to happen right now. Feeling like he would understand, I stood up a little to lean over and kiss his cheek and stroke his shoulder. I didn't say anything else about it, but I sat back down and dug out my phone.

"Do you mind if I take a picture of this beautiful food now?" I asked him.

He laughed, the sound a low rumble from his chest. "What's all this picture taking of food all the time? What's going on?"

I proceeded to tell him about Keisha and her Instagram idea, which led to showing him my page and all the food I had put up. My followers were growing, and people seemed to really like it.

A terrifying thought struck me. "You don't mind, do you? I should have thought to ask you. I don't list the name of your farm, but it does feature pretty prominently in the pictures."

Because it was Max, unsurprisingly, he didn't mind at all. He thought it was amazing, actually, and had some ideas about adding some pictures of the fields and of harvesting and washing some of the vegetables. He wanted to help me find some of the best spots when we were out walking with Benji.

***

"So, are we going to talk about this at all?" Max asked later as we strolled along the beach, watching the sun setting.

I sighed and leaned into his side. He wrapped his arm around me and pulled me close.

"I'm sorry. I know I can say that much at least. I'm not really sure how to explain."

"Was it Jessa? What happened there? Did she hurt you?"

"No. No, she didn't hurt me. She broke up with Jet. Or actually, Jet broke up with her. He's really the worst. He stole her rent money, and when she asked him about it, he turned everything on her, made her feel terrible, and left. She was devastated, which isn't like her at all. She really likes him for some reason. I have no idea why.

"Anyway, I really was just trying to help her calm down, keep her from going to confront him at the bar where he works, and get her to sober up and get some rest. It was going okay. I had gotten her to bed early in the morning and had gotten a little sleep myself, but her brother showed up."

"Her brother?"

"Yes. Ethan."

Max shifted our path to avoid the wave lapping the shoreline. "Wait a minute. Did he do something to you? He's the one who upset you?" he asked with an edge to his voice.

"He didn't do anything. It was all me." I fiddled with the button on my sweater. "Give me a second. It's hard to explain." I took some deep breaths and tried to put together a short version of the past that would help him understand a little of my history.

"So, Ethan and I … We sort of … dated."

"*Sort of*? What does that mean? When did this happen?"

"Max, this is old stuff. I haven't seen Ethan in years."

"Okay, but what does that mean – you dated, sort of?"

"So, you know I had to move in with Jessa's family, right? Well, they didn't love it. They are not a warm family, and they basically just tolerated me. That's totally fine. I was grateful. They don't owe me a single thing, but they allowed me to stay, and they absolutely did not need to do that. So, Ethan is a few years older, and we developed a 'thing,' I guess. I don't know how else to describe it. Ethan told me we couldn't be open about it because his family would be angry. It was a bad relationship or thing or whatever it was we had. When you called me innocent, you were wrong. I mean I … We—"

"I get it. I don't need to know more about … that. Wait. I do need to know. How much older is he?"

"Two years. Okay. So, it lasted mostly until he went away to college, but when he would come back, he would take back up with me. When Jessa and I moved out, I started to recognize that the relationship wasn't a good one, and I tried to distance myself. When he moved farther away after he finished college, I blocked him and worked hard to successfully avoid him when he came home to visit his family. It's worked for a long time. But he surprised me when he showed up yesterday morning at Jessa's. It was uncomfortable, but it was my fault I reacted so badly. It reminded me of when I was dependent on him and his family and how I felt about myself back then. It reminded me how much I have other voices in my head a lot telling me not great things about myself. It made me wonder how you could possibly want to be around me. How you could find anything good in me."

Max stopped us walking and pulled me in for a full hug. "Stop. I want to kill this guy already."

"It was a long time ago."

He looked at me for a moment and then slipped my sweater to the side a bit and began to dot kisses across my shoulder. "Don't doubt what I see in you. I see the truth – an amazing, talented, beautiful, sweet, sexy woman. That's who you are. I don't want to spend energy on this, but the amount of *frustration*, we'll call it, I have with Jessa and her family just grew exponentially. And it was already pretty big."

"Max."

"No. No excuses for those people. I'm glad you had somewhere to stay when you needed it, but I'm finding it difficult to find any gratitude toward anyone here. They had an opportunity to have you in their lives. They had an opportunity to help you. It should have been their honor."

I started to giggle. "Their honor to help me. Is that what it was?"

"Yes, goddammit," Max said, and I felt him smiling as he rested his face against the top of my head. "Their goddamn honor."

"Okay, Mad Max. Point made. You don't like the Michaud family."

"Right. I don't."

"But yesterday was my fault, and I'm sorry. I didn't mean to make you worry or feel bad or feel like you had to check up on me. I'm sorry I ruined your day, and I'm sorry Benji probably knew something was going on and was unhappy about it too."

"He was worried. We both were."

"I'm fine. I'll try really hard, okay? I have some bad patterns I fall into. I feel confident in my ability to take care of myself and get through things, but I don't have a lot of confidence in myself as far as being someone other people would want to be around."

"Well, we'll work on it because Benji and I definitely want to be around you. A lot."

***

I had some idea where things were headed between Max and me tonight. The touching was constant. All through dinner, walking along the beach, the entire ride home. It's like neither of us felt right unless we had some physical connection to each other. Benji wasn't home.

And Max was serious about me.

It blew my mind. Serious. About me.

We walked together up to my cottage, and I didn't hesitate to unlock the door to step inside with him. I was nervous, but I wasn't crazy. And I wasn't interested in playing games. At least, no games other than the ones I had been playing in my own mind, trying to convince myself I would survive a fling with Max Parker.

I asked if Max wanted any coffee or tea. I could tell he wasn't really interested in coffee or tea, but he said yes to either. Whatever I wanted.

It was a difficult transition. I didn't have a couch or a TV or anything for us to pretend to do to ease into this. I had a small kitchen table with two hard chairs and a bed. I got busy in the cramped kitchen area heating water for tea. Max stepped into the bathroom, and we traded places in the small space when he was done. We sat at the little table across from each other with our steaming cups of tea and started to laugh.

"We could go to my place," Max started, "but I have thought of you in this space so many times – this is basically a fantasy at this point."

"Your fantasy is to sit on hard chairs and have tea in the cottage with me?"

"My fantasy is to do pretty much anything in the cottage with you. But maybe you could come over here and have your tea?" he asked, patting his lap.

I pushed my tea to his side of the table and stood, edging around the corner until he reached out for my hand and pulled me down onto his thighs.

He pushed my sweater off one shoulder again. And then the other one. He said, "I still love this little dress," as he rubbed lazy patterns along the edge of my neck and kissed along my shoulder.

My skin was tingling. Every part of my body was humming, and I felt light-headed. "Max," I breathed out as his kisses built in intensity. I turned my face to him, and he caught my lips with his and tangled his fingers in my hair.

I pulled back and made intentional eye contact with him because I needed to tell him something. He had shared so much with me, and I always had my guard up. I needed him to know what I thought of him, how wonderful he was. When I pulled back to try to tell him, he kept stopping me by kissing me again. It was the sweetest torture, trying to fight against his kisses to tell him sweet things.

Finally, I braced my hands against his shoulders and pushed as hard as I could against his solid frame while balanced on his lap. "Max," I laughed. "Please, I want to tell you something."

He looked at me with happy, lazy eyes and said, "What's that, baby? What do you want to tell me?"

I kissed his cheek. "I want to tell you …" I kissed his other check. "I want to tell you that … you're wonderful." I kissed his nose. "I think you're the best man – the best person – I've ever met." I kissed each corner of his mouth. "You're the best father to Benji …" kiss, kiss, kiss "… and you're kind and thoughtful and strong and beautiful. And responsible. And just so amazing." Kiss, kiss, kiss. "I'm sorry," I said as I moved back again to look into his eyes. "I don't have all the words ready to tell you everything I feel, but I really feel, Max. So very much."

Max gripped my waist and stood up, pulling me up until he was carrying me. He walked the two steps to the bed and laid us down, still tangled arms and legs but lying next to each other on our sides facing each other. "Sweet Lanie," he said, stroking my face, then my hair, "I have dreamed of this so many nights." He lay on his back and pulled me on top of him.

And then it was everything. I felt all of him beneath me, and it felt so good.

His hands rubbed from my head down to the tops of my thighs – back and forth, stopping in between to stroke up my sides. His kisses were like a drug. I literally felt I could not get close enough to him. I was squirming, and he was groaning. Lips and tongues, hands and hips. We were seeking each other out in every way possible, and it was magic.

Until his phone buzzed on the table.

We froze and looked at each other. He was rock solid beneath me, and I was practically panting. After a beat, he said, "Forget it," and started to kiss me again. "This happened the last time I got to kiss you. It was nothing then, and it's nothing now."

"Max, we can't forget it. It could be Benji."

"You're right. Grrr. My brain cells are not working properly at the moment. Give me a second … Christ, you feel good." He kissed and stroked me as he slowly slid me off him and onto the bed. He stood to get his phone. "If this is Benji wanting to come home, I'm not having—"

"Max?" I asked. He stood like a statue looking at his phone.

He blinked a few times and then started patting his pockets to check for his wallet. He grabbed his keys from the table. "Uh – Benji," he said as he put his phone in his pocket and reached for his shoes.

"What, Max? What's going on?" I stood up and got my own shoes along with my sweater. "What's happening?"

"Benji. He's at the hospital."

Chapter 15

I sat in the waiting room tearing the magazine in my lap into tiny pieces. It started with one little corner I was worrying at absentmindedly, but now I had pages in shreds.

On the ride over Max had been stone silent. I wanted to know what was going on, but his demeanor invited nothing from me. It seemed like he didn't even know I had followed him and gotten in the truck with him to go to the hospital. I didn't know if Benji was hurt or sick. I didn't know if it was serious or something that would have him home in his own bed tonight.

I knew it wasn't an overreaction on Max's part. No matter what was going on, any time Benji ended up at the hospital was a moment that needed all of Max's attention and focus. Still, it seemed bigger than that. He wasn't present at all. He was ashen, and I thought I even saw his hands shaking as he started the truck.

We were halfway to the hospital when I started to realize the other piece at play in this crisis.

Claudia.

Max had described that as a headache, a trip to the hospital, and her being gone all within twenty-four hours. That kind of trauma had to be life-altering. This moment made me appreciate even more who he was and how he handled himself. And made my heart ache even more for him. I tried not to take on that layer of the worry for Benji. I tried to be practical and assure myself that he was likely fine and that it wasn't something overly serious. That was probable. Little boys got sick and hurt. It happened, and it usually wasn't a big deal. Max didn't need to deal with any of my anxiousness on top of his own, so I tried very hard to be calm next to him, offering whatever silent support I could.

For what that was worth.

And it didn't feel like it was worth much, especially with Max seeming to not notice I was even there.

I didn't have to wait long once we got to the hospital to know that Benji was going to be okay. Max's dad had come out to meet us when we first arrived. He had quickly let us know that Benji had been running through the house and slipped turning a corner. He had hit his head on the base of a nearby bookcase and gotten a gash above his left eye that needed stitches. I expected Max to express some relief, but he was as tense as ever and didn't spare me a glance as he went with his dad to see Benji. His dad looked back at me as they walked away and said, "We'll keep you posted, but don't worry. He's okay." Mr. Parker put his arm around a dazed Max as they walked away.

Max's parents finally came into the waiting room to let me know Benji was doing well a little later on. Mr. Parker said Benji was asking to see me and told me the nurse would meet me to take me back. Mrs. Parker looked disapproving as I threw my pile of magazine paper shreds in the trash and walked toward the patient room entrance.

"Benji?" I said as I pushed aside the curtain a bit and approached his bed.

"Lady Lanie! Look at my cool stitches. Daddy told me I look like Frankenstein Jr."

"Ah, Benji," I brushed his hair away from his face. "You look super tough, but are you okay? Is it hurting?" I looked across Benji's bed up to Max. His face was softer now, but he looked exhausted. "Are you okay?" I mostly mouthed.

I went to the other side of Benji's bed and put my arm around Max's middle and squeezed him toward me. I took Benji's little hand in mine and held it tight.

Benji did look a little like Frankenstein Jr. He had about four stitches starting in his left eyebrow and pointing outward away from his eye. Thinking about what could have

happened if he had hit his eye – just a half inch or so over …
Well, I didn't want to think about it.

"There was all this blood, Lanie. Grammie cried a
bunch and Grampie drove real fast. I cried too. But I'm okay
now. The doctor had this cool puppet and I get to keep him!
He got stitches too!" Benji pulled a stuffed doll from under
his sheet. The little doll had some yarn stitched near his
eyebrow to match Benji's stitches.

I looked up and smiled at Max. I pulled him to me
again and tried to reassure him. "He's good," I quietly
murmured to Max. "He's okay."

The nurse came into the space and told Benji they
were going to go for a little ride and that he could bring his
puppet. She told him they were going to get a CT scan, which
was just taking a picture inside his head.

"Inside my head?" Benji asked incredulously. "Cool!
Can Lanie and Daddy come to watch?"

"They need to stay here," the nurse said as she helped
Benji shift from the bed to the wheelchair. "But it should
only take a few minutes." She looked at Max, who had
flinched when she mentioned the scan, and said, "It's just a
precaution. Nothing at all to worry about, and we really will
be right back."

I turned fully to Max after they left and tried to hug him. He was so tense that it was difficult. He lifted his arms enough to return the hug, but he was still not really with me. I put my hands up to his checks and stretched up on my tiptoes to give him a kiss. "He's okay, Max," I said between soft kisses. I tried to infuse as much peace and calm into those kisses as I could. My heart was breaking seeing him go through this.

He slowly started to wake up a bit at a time. Returning the kisses after the fourth or fifth one. "It's just … when Claudia …" he said and trailed off.

"I know," I said as I hugged him close and pressed the side of my face against his chest. "I know," I said again. "I thought of that as we were driving over. I can't imagine what this is like for you, But, Max, he's good. The CT scan is going to be fine, and he's already loving showing off his stitches. It could have been worse, but it wasn't. He's all right, thank God."

Max relaxed into me, and we hugged until we were interrupted by his mother. "Where's Benji?" she said, coming into the little room.

I stepped away from Max and told them I was going to go find the bathroom. "Would you like some water or hot tea? Anything at all?"

Max looked at me and gave me a small smile. "That would be great, Lanie. Whatever they have. Thanks." Then he turned to his mom and started to explain about the CT scan while I made my exit.

***

"She follows you around like a stray puppy. You have to see this is bad for Benji."

I had returned with the water and heard Mrs. Parker's words through the curtain as I approached. They stung like a slap to the face. I had been serious when I told Max I didn't expect her to like me. But there was a big difference between knowing that was true and hearing her express what she really thought about me. And to hear not only her dislike for me but that she thought I was actually bad for Benji as well …

"You can't fix this, Max. Her self-worth is unhealthy and you're not improving that. You're taking advantage—"

"Christ, Mom. Taking advantage? Is that what you really think?" Max's tone was hushed but his voice still carried clearly into the hallway.

"You know what I mean, Max. You will steamroll that girl. She looks at you like you're a god. And maybe a meal ticket."

"Mom. Jesus, where is this coming from? I've never known you to be like this. *That girl* is not looking for a handout or a savior. She has taken care of herself for a long time and has done a damn good job. I mean, yeah, she's young, and she struggles with some things. She's—"

"She's looking for a parent. She's looking for someone to fill her up. She's empty inside. Max, that can't be you. You have Benji to think about. First, Claudia and now this … this girl. Benji has to come first."

"Excuse me!" The voice behind me was startling, and I dropped the bottle of water I was holding. "I'm just bringing Benji back from his scan," the nurse said as she opened the curtain.

Max and his mom looked at me standing there. Benji was talking about the CT machine, but no one was listening. Everything sounded muffled, and both Max and his mom looked at me and the water on the floor, realizing I had been standing there as they were talking.

"I'm … I think I'm going to sit out in the waiting room for now if that's okay."

"Lanie, wait a minute," Max started, but I was already making my way down the hall.

***

I really didn't want to do this. I considered calling Jessa or even Keisha to get a ride home from the hospital – well, a ride back to the farm. I really didn't want to see Max's mom anymore or talk to Max about their conversation. I had no idea what he was going to say. When he was talking to her, it had sounded like he was about to agree with her at least to some extent.

And why wouldn't he?

I didn't want to be a burden. I knew his mom was wrong comparing me to Claudia. At least that was one thing I knew for sure – I loved Benji and Max. I did. There was no "falling in love" or "really liking" in my case. I adored and loved both of them. It hurt my heart to think of causing either of them pain or hardship. I hated Claudia for what she had done to them. I knew Benji was probably too young to have felt it, but I had simmering, guilt-ridden anger for a dead woman because of her feelings (or lack thereof) for Benji.

But Pam Parker wasn't wrong that I was a mess. And I was a burden. What did I bring to the table except the love I had for them? And all I was doing was stressing Max out because it was obvious he was not used to being at odds with his mom.

I was trying to fight the slide into my default negative place – thinking I was worthless and a burden, but it was really hard. I kept trying because Max had made it really clear that he was serious about me. That was so important and surprising. And I knew that, because of the way he felt about me, spiraling into my own pity party would make things harder on him. He had his mom and everything with Benji. He didn't need to have to worry about my feelings on top of that.

That's why I didn't call for a ride. It would have been something else for Max to worry about if he came out with Benji and found me gone.

But I really, really wanted to be gone.

Instead, I sat quietly in the waiting room with Mr. Parker until Max, Benji, and Mrs. Parker came out through the double doors. Benji ran over to me and hopped up on my lap. "Lanie, they took a picture of my head. It was so cool. But they didn't let me see the picture."

"Everything all clear?" I asked, looking up at Max.

He nodded at me gravely. "He's totally fine. Saved by his hard head," he said as he stroked Benji's hair.

"Good, that's really good." I snuggled Benji to me a bit more. "Ready to go home, buddy?" I wanted to kick myself. There was that stupid word again. *Home.*

I glanced at Mrs. Parker to see what she thought of me calling it that. She just continued looking at Benji with a worried look on her face.

"Yes, let's head home," Max said, putting his hand out to me. Benji held tightly to my neck as I stood up with Max's help and kept Benji in my arms. He was heavy to carry, but it had been a big night and he was wiped out. He was being especially cuddly, and I was not going to tell him he had to walk when he wanted to snuggle.

When we got to Max's truck, Mrs. Parker tried to take Benji from me to hug him and strap him into his seat, but he wouldn't let go of me. She did not like that at all. She settled on giving him a kiss and rubbing his back, but she pointedly reminded Max for the tenth time to let her know if he needed any help with Benji over the next few days.

Benji fell asleep on the way home, and it wasn't long before Max got to work trying to make me feel better. Which actually just made me feel terrible. It was further proof that I was a burden – something for him to take care of.

"It's totally fine, Max. I told you before, I don't expect your mom to like me, and I'm really okay with that. I would feel the same way in her situation."

"Damnit, Lanie, please don't say that. There's no reason for her to not like you and no reason for you to be okay with it."

"I'm good, Max. Let's just focus on getting Benji home and not worry about this right now. It's not important."

"It is! The look on your face when the nurse opened the curtain. It does hurt your feelings. I mean, of course, it does. I just want you to know that I will fix it. This isn't like my mom … I just don't get it."

Max was just being Max – trying to fix it. Trying to take care of me. Trying to build me up. But I didn't want that. He was doing his thing, but there was an edge of frustration. The edge was the same I had seen from him when Jessa had hit his truck with Benji inside. Of course, there was lots of anger that day to go along with it, but there was that worry and tension in the set of his jaw. He was the one who needed to be taken care of right now, but he wouldn't allow it. Every time I tried to deflect or shift the focus away from me, he brought it right back around.

Eventually we both just fell silent. I held his hand, but we didn't have much more to say to each other. I didn't think

Max even noticed we had just stopped talking. His mind was still frazzled, and it felt like the best thing to do was just let him be.

While I wanted to help when we got back to the farm, I could see Max wouldn't have been able to focus solely on Benji if I had. He had a right and a need to do that, so I just kissed his cheek and rubbed Benji's head as Max carried him in to take him to his bed.

Chapter 16

The next few days were … okay. There was a tentativeness that was unexpected considering how amazing our date had been. I was still fighting against my insecurities, and Max was battling his shock and worry. I could only imagine how the trauma of how his wife had died impacted his reaction to situations like this.

Benji was happy but a little subdued. We all fell into our usual routines, but without the spark we usually had. I had really been trying to be positive and upbeat, despite all the doubts I was having, but I was beginning to come to the conclusion that, although Max had been seriously considering a relationship with me, Benji's accident had changed things. It, understandably, was making him reconsider his priorities. Inviting anyone else into his life took some of his attention away from Benji. That was clear in some of the choices he was making about how he was spending his time.

While I was washing the dishes after the farm lunch on the Friday after Benji's injury, Max hung back once everyone had cleared out, but it wasn't to spend time with me.

"I think I'm going to knock off early today and take Benji into town for ice cream. You should take the rest of the day off. I know you have to work this weekend, so you could use the rest. My crew has things handled the rest of the day."

"Ice cream, Dad? Really? I want a double dipper, okay?" Benji hopped back and forth as he rattled off the different flavors of ice cream, changing his mind as quickly as he changed which foot he landed on.

"Great," I said, trying to keep the strain out of my voice. "That sounds like …" Sounds like what? Fun? A good time? Anything I thought to say sounded like I was either sulking that I wasn't going with them, or I was fishing for an invitation. "That sounds like … a good idea," I finally finished.

"All right, Benji. Let's go get cleaned up and then head out."

"Daddy, isn't Lanie coming with us?" Benji came over and hugged my leg.

"Sorry, Benji, I need to finish up here, and you and your dad should go have some *man time*." I tried to make it sound fun and lighthearted by deepening my voice as low as it would go as I said "man time." "I have some things I need to take care of, so this will be good for everyone."

Benji squeezed my leg again, but ice cream called, and he was excited. It wasn't long before he released me and skipped over to this dad. I called out a cheerful goodbye and tried hard to keep the frozen smile on my face until they left the barn.

***

After an evening spent in tears, followed by a sleepless night, I had pretty much decided this wasn't going to work. My time on the farm was winding down with just a few weeks left before the students would leave. It was time for me to do what was best for Max and Benji, and that meant it was time to give Max an out. He deserved to find a partner who made his life easier, not harder. Someone who didn't need building up and taking care of. Someone his mom was happy to see him with. Someone who brought more to the table.

Not me.

I told him as much when I got back from my shift at the coffee shop the next evening. He came out to meet me just outside his door as I walked from my car to the cottage.

"Hi, sweetheart," he said reaching out to me.

I felt grubby in my work shirt that was splattered with coffee and milk, and my hair was falling out of its ponytail. I greedily took in his form in his faded jeans, T-shirt, and bare feet.

"Hi, Max," I said letting him take my hand and pull me toward him a bit.

I did not want to do this. But it really was best for him, so I took a deep breath and went to that place inside myself where I didn't feel anything. The place I went when my mom left and when Ethan would tell me the reasons I needed to be kept a secret.

"Lanie, baby, I missed you this week." He looked so tired, and all I wanted to do was comfort him and pet him and make him feel better.

Okay, I told myself. *One more kiss. You can just take one more kiss from him.*

He leaned down and tenderly kissed my lips. "I'm sorry I've been distracted. The thing with Benji – it just rattled me. I'm sorry I haven't been there for you." He kissed me again.

This was agony. One more kiss wasn't helping at all. Time was up. I knew I needed to do this no matter how hard it was.

I leaned away from him. "Max, I think … I think we should cool things off."

Max went from a lazy expression to a stunned one.

"This week was a lot," I continued. "It was a reminder for both of us about what's really important. And that's Benji."

Max stiffened and dropped his arms from where they had been holding me. "What are you talking about, Lanie?" He looked at me with a confused expression. "What the hell do you mean?

"I mean," I began, "you shouldn't have to think about being there for me. You shouldn't have to think about anything but Benji at a time like this. That's the way it should be. I'm a distraction from that – another responsibility for you. I don't want to feel like a burden. I don't want you to feel torn."

"Damnit, Lanie. Stop it. We've talked about this. It's true. This was a tough week. And it's true, I felt torn. The things my mom said … well, they sucked. I don't know how to fix that situation. And she also fucked with my head – thinking I was taking advantage of you. That's what's been kicking around in my brain. But that doesn't make you a burden. That makes this real life. You're not a burden. Please come inside. Benji's finishing his show. I can't stay out here much longer. He'd love to see you. And I would, too. Please just come in."

"Not tonight, Max." God, this was killing me. "I think we have to start thinking about when this summer is over. I don't want it to be too hard on Benji when I leave."

"When you leave?"

I had seen Max angry a lot of times in the time I'd known him, so it wasn't unfamiliar. But it really hurt to see him that way now. Knowing I was doing it to him. I knew he had real feelings for me, and I knew I was hurting him. But this was going to hurt us all a lot more if I didn't stop it now.

"Max, we can talk some more later. Go on back in to Benji. You'll see that I'm right when you think it over."

Max didn't say anything more. But he showed a lot of restraint in not slamming the door behind him when every tense muscle in his body said he wanted to tear the door off its hinges.

***

Things were not going well. This wasn't a surprise, but it reminded me yet again how hard hope was to kill. I had zero reason to hope for something better than this pain. I had known it was coming, but apparently, somewhere deep inside me there was that glimmer of hope I had been ignoring. But, as painful as it was watching things with Max die, it was harder seeing *him* in pain over it.

"I can take over with Benji after farm lunch today," he said before leaving the house a few mornings later. He had been doing this more and more – only having me work or watch Benji when he absolutely needed me to. Benji was excited to spend more time with his dad, but he often asked if we could all hang out together. Max and I found ourselves talking over each other to explain to Benji why we couldn't – I needed to prepare for work at the coffee shop or run some errands or basically anything either of us could think of in that moment.

"I'm fine to watch him all afternoon," I said to him as I poured some coffee in his travel cup. "I don't have to work tonight."

"No," he returned. "Like you said, we need to think about Benji. He needs to get used to the idea of you not being around."

This was a new Max. I had been around the dragon Max and the incredibly kind and affectionate Max. This was vacant Max. It was like he had taken a page from my book and emptied himself out. For the first time, I understood what this could feel like on the receiving end. Really terrible. It was like he didn't care about anything. Like he didn't care about me. Or even himself.

Benji was feeling it, too. He had been cranky, and it had nothing to do with his stitches. He was still pretty proud of those, showing them to all the students and farmworkers with a description of how much blood there had been when it happened.

"Max, please don't be upset about this. We knew it was coming. I just – I care about you and Benji. I'm not trying to make this harder."

"You care about us?" he asked incredulously. There was angry Max. No hiding that emotion now. "You care about us so much you want to end things before they even start?" Emotion flashed across his face. "Lanie, please, this doesn't make sense—"

"Hi, Lanie," Benji said as he walked into the kitchen. "Are we baking something today?" he asked without his usual enthusiasm.

"Hi, Benji buddy." I reached down to him for a hug. "How about we make some brownies? How does that sound?"

"Ooh," he said, perking up a little. "I love brownies!"

***

"What is happening?" Keisha asked later that day as I washed dishes in the barn. We had finished farm lunch and Max had taken Benji back to the house.

"What do you mean?" I asked, looking over at her.

"All the moping. You, Max, Benji. Everybody's moping. I haven't seen you eat all week."

"It's nothing really. I mean Benji had the thing with his injury and that's been stressful and—"

"Benji is fine. Don't blame this on that. This is definitely *not* that. Did you and Max break up?"

"We were never really together," I whispered as I tried to will my eyes to stop tearing up.

"You were!" Keisha insisted. "You've been hanging out for weeks. And he had you over to his house and you went out to that dinner."

"No, Keisha. We weren't together – not really. We were thinking about it, I guess, but it can't happen. It's just too complicated with Benji. And I'm a problem Max doesn't need. He has so much to deal with. I'm a mess, and he doesn't need to take care of me or worry about me on top of that."

Keisha threw down the dishtowel she had started using to dry the plates as I washed them. "In what universe are you a mess, Lanie? You have your shit together better than practically anyone I know."

Keisha always ran hot with her emotions, and she sounded a little mad. Like I was trying her patience. I felt terrible. I realized I was going to lose her, too. These new friends had tolerated me when I had a role to play in their lives, but this was all coming to an end. And these fragile relationships were not going to survive.

"You did this, Lanie? You called things off with Max? Why would you do that? He's crazy about you. Why would you do this to him? To yourself?"

I didn't have anything to say. Literally nothing. What could I say to her? That I didn't deserve him? Or her concern? I had already said as much, and she was just getting madder, so I just shrugged.

"Lanie, that's not fair. You don't just get to decide for other people. You're blocking Max out and deciding for him that he shouldn't be with you. I think you're already blocking me out, too. It's selfish and cowardly. And you know what?" She was getting more and more worked up as she talked. "Maybe you're right. If this is how you treat people who care about you … maybe we are better off." She walked out of the barn without another word. And without a look back.

***

I frequently spent a lot of time thinking negative thoughts about myself, but I generally did try to avoid feeling sorry for myself. I felt lots of things I shouldn't feel, and I dwelt on them, fixated on them. I cried and I got down on myself and I said pretty terrible things to myself. Things I would never say to another person. Things I would never even think about another person. I knew my confidence sucked, and I knew I found it hard to believe other people would see any value in me.

But I really tried hard not to fall into the self-pity trap. The "why me" trap. I accepted that I didn't have many people in my life, but it was always easy to remind myself how things could be worse. To remind myself that I had lots of things to be grateful for – my job, a place of my own (sort of, until recently anyway), food and clothes and all the things I had learned not to take for granted.

So, as I beat myself up that night in the little cottage, I wasn't asking "why me?" But I was asking "why them?" Why did they have to be subjected to me? Why did I have the power to mess up their lives or hurt their feelings?

I thought a lot about Keisha's comment. That I had my shit together. What did that mean? I was a mess. I tried to imagine what Keisha saw when she said that. I guess she saw someone who was generally hardworking, content, happy even – for *most* of this summer. Someone who could take care of Benji and the house and feeding the students. I guess that's what she saw, and when I thought about it, that made me glad. I was kind of capable, and that made me feel good that someone like Keisha would see that and think it was a positive thing. So how was I a mess? I kept asking myself that question because I knew that I was.

I was a mess *on the inside.*

A total ugly, pathetic, intolerable burden of a mess. I didn't need therapy to know where these feelings came from. I never knew my dad. I didn't even know who he was, and he obviously had no interest in me. My mom didn't love me. She resented the burden I presented even though she did very little to take care of me. And the only people I had to rely on, until recently, saw me as a drag, a dirty secret, an inconvenience. So, maybe I didn't feel sorry for what I had, but I did feel sorry for what I was. I was one massive pity party in that respect. I wouldn't want to be around myself, so how could anyone else want to be?

I thought about the people in my life who had shaped how I felt about myself – my mom, Ethan, Jessa. I thought about all the other people I had kept at arm's length because of how I felt about myself. How I never became friends with anyone other than Jessa at school or anyone at work. And I thought about how that had been different this summer. How Benji and Max and Keisha ... Rich and even the other students had warmed up to me as the summer progressed. Other than Max's mom, no one seemed to think I was horrible to be around. No one was rushing to get away from me or making comments about me to remind me what they thought about me.

It wasn't like this was the first time I had considered this, but my experience these last few months really made me think about the people who had me think this way about myself. It really made me focus on how it was possible their words and actions said a lot more about them than they said about me. Again, I didn't need therapy to make these connections, but I was realizing maybe I needed some help to make those thoughts stick. To make those good thoughts crowd out the bad ones.

And maybe letting good people in could be part of that help.

I jerked the covers angrily as I turned on my side in the bed and suddenly felt like I was going to be sick. I was hurting Max and Benji and Keisha for no good reason. I was taking the things my mom had made me feel about myself and imposing those thoughts onto everyone else.

I needed to see Max. I needed to apologize to Keisha. I needed to try to make this work. I needed to do it for these people I loved … And, it was hard to admit to myself, but I also needed to do it for me. I could try so hard to make Max's mom warm up to me. I just wanted to see him. Right now.

Unfortunately, it was late, and I knew Benji was already in bed. I thought about texting Max, but that wasn't how I wanted to fix things. I wanted to touch him. Tell him how sorry I was and beg him to give me another chance. And I would do it – first thing in the morning. I wouldn't let myself change my mind or let doubt creep in.

And to make sure, I needed to take some action now. I grabbed my phone and sent a text to Keisha.

11:30pm: *I'm sorry, Keisha. You were totally right. I don't want to push you out. You have been the best friend I could ever have imagined. I'm so sorry. I'm going to talk to Max tomorrow. You really made me think about things. Thank you for being you.* ❤

I saw three dots on my phone appear and disappear, so I knew Keisha was awake and had seen my message.

11:35pm: *No worries, girl. It's all good. And I overreacted. As usual. Stop stressing and get some sleep.* ❤

I smiled as I snuggled under the covers. Simple as that. I apologized, and she accepted. Jessa would have tortured me and gotten something in return for the forgiveness.

I lay there, thinking of the things I would say to Max in the morning. Hoping to go to sleep quickly so morning would come sooner. When there was a sudden knock at my door, my heart leapt.

Could I be so lucky? Was Max coming to see me for some reason? How did he know? I jumped out of bed and quickly opened the door.

I wasn't that lucky. Not only was it not Max, but it was practically the last person on earth I wanted to see.

Ethan.

I stood in my tank top and sleep shorts, wishing I had put on more clothes. Ethan looked me up and down and reached for a lock of my hair. "Hi, pixie stick."

"Ethan, wh— what are you doing here?" I stepped away from his reach while still trying to block the doorway. I did not want to invite him inside.

"Jessa told me you were here. I wanted to see you, pixie. Come on. Let me in."

"No, Ethan," I said, maybe for the first time ever. "I don't want to see you. I want you to go."

"Come on, pixie. I know you have to have been missing me. No one else would want this skinny little ass. How long has it been? You have to be dying for it."

"Ethan, please. Just leave."

"Now … me?" Ethan said trying to nudge me further inside the cottage, "I'm used to you, little pixie stick. I'm so used to you, it's a habit. An addiction, you might even say. I need you, pixie. You owe me for all the times you've ignored my texts and calls. All the times I could have had your scrawny ass."

In that moment, I could see clearly that Ethan's poisonous words were only meant as a weapon. It would have been obvious to anyone else, but I had always taken his words as truths about me.

But now? He was trying to manipulate me. It was so clear to me now that, instead of making me feel small and vulnerable, it made me feel angry and brave.

I pushed Ethan as forcefully as I could with both hands against his shoulders. "I want you to leave, Ethan!"

My shove didn't have much strength behind it, but I had the element of surprise on my side. Since Ethan wasn't expecting that reaction from me at all, he was caught off balance and it pushed him back a few steps. He ended up on the porch closer to the steps instead of the door. I stepped out on the porch as well and told him again to leave.

Ethan snarled and grunted as he grabbed both my forearms and began to squeeze. There would definitely be bruises. He knew what he was doing. He pulled me toward him, holding me in place by putting pressure on my arms, which he held at my sides. He forced his horrible, toxic mouth to mine. I turned my head from side to side to try to avoid his foul kisses.

He responded by holding both my arms with one of his hands and gripping my face with his other. He again forced his mouth to mine as he tightened his hold with his fingers like a vise. I struggled and fought against him but couldn't shake his grip.

"Come on, pixie. You know this just turns me on more. Go ahead. Fight me," he said, roughly pressing his lips to mine again.

I knew it was likely to make things worse, but I couldn't stand him kissing me a second more, and I wasn't making any progress shaking him off. As the bile rose in my throat, I clenched my eyes shut and bit down on his lip. Hard.

He instantly drew back. "What the fuck, pixie?" he yelled. He touched his finger to the blood on his lip and grimaced before opening the same hand and backhanding me across the face. It knocked me off balance, so I was confused for a second about the next sounds I heard.

Stomping. A loud crack. Shouting. And finally, once I regained my balance and saw what was happening, I could match the sound with Ethan being thrown from the porch.

Max looked ready to kill. The fire-breathing dragon was back, and he made the one I had met so many months ago look like a baby dragon. This one was glorious in his anger. Majestic and splendid and strong.

"I'm calling the police," he said to Ethan who was trying to scramble himself up off the ground.

"No, man. No way. She fucking bit me."

"And you slapped her. I saw it all. I'm calling the police. And Lanie is getting a restraining order. And I'm getting a trespassing order. You don't want me to ever see you again. Ever. I mean it. Now get the fuck off my land."

Ethan looked at me. "You fucking bitch. You stupid little cunt, I'm going to—"

Max roared as he flew off the porch at Ethan. He punched him, knocking him to the ground again. Ethan was grabbing his nose, which was bleeding freely.

"Ethan, just leave. Please," I said as I approached Max. "Max," I said as I touched his taut arm. "Please. Let's just let him leave. I don't want you to get into trouble. Please, Max."

"Out, you motherfucker," Max said in a deadly tone.

Ethan didn't make the same mistake this time. He muttered a string of obscenities, but he did it walking down the path to his car.

"Daddy? Lanie?" Benji stood at the door to his house, eyes as big as saucers. Milo stood beside him.

I rubbed Max's arms and shoulders, trying to relax him. Bring him back to the present. He shook his head a few times, then looked at me. "Okay?" he asked, as if he couldn't find more words. He was running his finger along the cheek Ethan had struck, looking murderous.

"I'm fine, Max. Really, I'm okay. Let's go get Benji back inside."

We walked toward Benji, and I was the one who picked him up and assured him everything was fine as we went into the house. Max still had so much energy. It was rolling off him in waves, and he needed some time to bring his adrenaline levels down.

"Who was that, Lanie? Why did Daddy hit him?"

"That was a bad man, Benji. Your daddy was protecting us. That bad man won't come back ever again. Okay? I'm sorry he was so loud and scary. Your daddy took care of it though. And we're going to tell the police and then they will take care of it. He won't come back. I promise."

I would never have dreamed of calling the police about Ethan before, but there was Benji and Max to think about now. Ethan needed to stay away for good. I would do everything Max had told him we would do. I would tell the police, and I would get the restraining order. I didn't care what Jessa or her family thought.

"It's late and you need to get some sleep, buddy," I said, stroking Benji's back.

"I'm not tired ," he whined. I could believe it. He had just seen his dad attack another man. I'm sure he wouldn't be able to sleep for a little while.

"Okay, let's have some hot chocolate and watch one episode of your show. Your daddy could use some hot chocolate, too. How does that sound?"

Benji perked up at this idea and wriggled out of my arms and onto the couch, inviting Milo up to serve as his pillow.

Chapter 17

"I did not think I would end the day in your bed," I said as I shyly slid into the bed next to Max.

"Come closer," he urged as he pulled me to him.

Benji had finally settled down and had fallen asleep on the couch. Max had taken him upstairs and put him into his bed, and Milo had quickly cuddled up to him again.

Then, in an unspoken agreement, Max had taken my hand and walked me to his bedroom. He found me a new toothbrush, and we took turns in his small bathroom getting ready for bed. I still had on my sleep shorts and tank top under an oversized sweatshirt Max had given me when we were sitting on the couch with Benji. I had pulled it off after brushing my teeth and felt Max watching me walk to the bed.

"I'm not sure how to stop wanting to go kill that guy," Max said, the anger still palpable. "I know that's not what you need right now." He let out a frustrated breath. "I'm really trying."

"It's okay for it to be about what you need right now, Max. That was a lot. I'm so sorry Benji saw any of it. I'm sorry you did, too."

"Lanie," he pulled back just enough to be able to look at my face, "are you really okay?" He stroked and then kissed the red part of my cheek Ethan had struck. Then he pulled my arms from under the covers and looked at where the bruising was just starting to show along my forearms.

Max had called a friend of his who worked at the local police station while I had been sitting with Benji. He had explained the situation and grown even more upset when his friend told him there wasn't a lot that would come of them picking Ethan up, but if we wanted that to happen, I would need to go to the police station to file my report. He said Ethan was likely to be released and would probably be let off with a fine because it would be considered a low-level assault. I had seen Max nearly crush his phone and later understood it had been at the words "low level." His friend also told him that it was fine to wait until the following day to file the report if we weren't looking to have Ethan picked up right away. I had quickly agreed to waiting, although it still upset Max. I didn't want to make this night any harder for Max or Benji than it already had been. And I was pretty concerned that Max might be seen to have assaulted Ethan even though he was only trying to defend me.

Max's jaw clenched tightly as he stroked the inside of my forearm.

"Max," I said, pulling my arms away and putting them back under the blankets. "Don't think about that right now. I'm fine. Really." I reached for his hand and pulled it into mine. "And I want to tell you something."

"There's more?" Max looked pained.

"No, Max. This is something different. And I need to tell you, and you have to believe me."

"Of course I'll believe you. Why wouldn't I believe you?"

I realized I was biting my lip when Max reached up and pulled it free. "Lanie, what is it?"

"I just want you to know – really know – that I was going to fix it in the morning. Or try to fix it anyway. Before Ethan ever showed up. Before you came out and ... and ..."

"What were you going to fix? What do you mean?"

"I was trapped in the idea that I was going to make your life harder. When I heard your mom say that I was bad for Benji ..."

"That's bullshit," Max exclaimed. "And it's not what she said. I don't think. I'll talk to her. I just don't get what's going on with her."

"Max, it's okay. Really. That one was hard for me, but I thought about it a lot and, while I'm still struggling to understand what I can bring to a relationship with you, I know that I'm not bad for Benji. I love him so much. I'm not a bad influence or anything, so I don't know how I could be bad for him. I know I'm not …" I trailed off. "But that's not the point," I picked up again. "The point is, I was dwelling on this idea of making your life harder. Of being a burden to you. Of driving a wedge between you and your mom. Of you realizing or agreeing with your mom that I'm kind of empty or needy or—"

"Stop," Max interrupted. "You are the least needy person I've ever met, and it actually drives me crazy. I need you to need me. I told you before. It makes me happy to take care of you. Even if you don't need it, I wish you would let me." He wrapped his arm around my waist and pulled me even closer into him.

"I'm going to. I mean that's what I'm trying to say. I know the people in my life are the ones who have made me what I am. And I don't like the people in my life." Max stiffened. "Not you, silly. I'm talking about my mom and Ethan and even Jessa."

"I like what you are. Who you are. And I hate that girl."

"Max. Focus." I luxuriated in the freedom I had to reach out and run my fingers through his short hair. "What I realized is that I can't trust what they said about me. Said to me. They weren't fair to me. They weren't kind. And I've seen that isn't how it should be. You and the people you surround yourself with have shown me that. I can't promise I won't let those voices get to me again and again. But I decided that I had to tell you – well, I had to tell you that I love you. And I have to let you decide if you're willing to live with my love. Let you decide if it's a burden or a problem to solve."

Max wiped away the tear that was leaking from my eye toward my pillow.

"Lanie," Max swallowed and cleared his throat. "Lanie, your love is the sweetest gift. Never a burden or a problem. An unexpected, beautiful gift that I'm so lucky to receive." He stopped to touch his lips to mine. "Lanie, baby, I love you so damn much." He kept the kisses coming. "So fucking beautiful." His finger trailed against the side of my breast. "So fucking sweet." He shifted his thigh between my legs. "So fucking strong," he said, and I started to feel tingly – every nerve ending buzzing. "So fucking good."

He slipped his hand under my shirt and rubbed all over, stroking and teasing as I tried to restrain myself from bearing down on his thigh. My body was tingling and burning, and all I wanted was to be closer to Max.

"That's right, baby," he said to me. "Take what you need." He pulled me even closer and lapped at my neck and down my chest.

Beyond reason, I wriggled and squirmed against him until I suddenly just fell apart. "That's right, baby," I could hear Max's reassuring voice as he petted and stroked my hair. "Such a good girl. Such a beautiful girl."

"Max," I tried to bring myself out of the lovely haze I was in. I needed to make him feel good. I needed to—

"You stay right here, baby," he said as he cradled me into himself. "Close your pretty eyes and rest. You've had a long day, sweetheart."

There was no escaping it when he kept cuddling me and stroking me and saying such adoring things in his gravelly voice. Sleep took me in the sweetest way, cradled in Max's confident embrace all night.

***

"So ... he's gone?" Max asked.

We were sitting in his kitchen waiting for his parents to arrive. It was Friday night – a few nights after the incident with Ethan. Max insisted on a do-over date and his parents were coming to pick Benji up for a sleepover. I was embarrassed at the idea of facing Mr. and Mrs. Parker. I mean, everyone knew why Max would want Benji to sleep over. But I reminded myself, this was an adult relationship. This was normal. What wasn't normal was my past with Ethan – full of secrets and shame.

"Gone," I said, picking up my cup of tea for a sip. I had bought a new dress for our date, and I knew Max liked the yellow sundress as much as the lavender one because he had stood speechless, his mouth hanging open for a few seconds, when he opened the door. The fact that he felt this way about me – that he felt this attraction to me – continued to take me by surprise.

I had spent the last few nights staying with him at his insistence. He would not allow me to sleep in the cottage, knowing Ethan could come back. Benji had taken the change in stride, and I had somehow controlled myself and resisted using his gorgeous body the way I had that first night. But the cuddling and kissing had already become a delicious habit.

"Yes, Jessa called asking me about my half of the rent again." I rolled my eyes and Max smiled. "And she said Ethan moved away for good. That he told her he hated it here, and if she ever wanted to see him again, she would have to go to him. She also said he had fallen and broken his nose." I looked at Max pointedly.

"Fallen? Is that what happened?" Max stretched his legs out and crossed his ankles. "That sounds about right."

After filing my police report, Max's police officer friend had let Max know they had tried to go pick Ethan up for questioning but hadn't found him at home. Now we knew why. I sincerely hoped he was gone for good. But even if he came back, I knew he couldn't hurt me anymore. Max wouldn't allow me to be vulnerable in that way again. He had spent every free second of the last few days reassuring me – feeding me with enough praise and love to push out some of the cruel voices I was used to. I knew it wasn't a permanent solution to all of my issues and insecurities, but it sure was working in the short-term.

"You're not going back to live with Jessa," he said matter-of-factly.

"No. No, you're right. I'm not," I said, worried about the next part of this conversation. We hadn't yet discussed what was happening when the season ended. "But I have another option," I started.

"Of course you do."

"No, Max. I mean, another option for an apartment. I asked about a studio apartment a little while ago … when things were … Anyway, I got a response that it's available again. Thanks to this summer, I can afford it, and I think I should go take a look."

"What the hell?" Max whispered, looking toward the hallway where we expected Benji to appear any moment. "No. No apartment." He stood up and paced around the kitchen. He was mentally counting to ten or imagining calming mantras or something because he clearly was trying to bring down his energy. It was such a dad thing – such a protective thing. He looked at me and softened his expression. He pulled his chair closer to me and sat down again.

"Don't leave," he said, fiddling with his cup. "Please stay here with us. I want you here in the house, but I'll live with it if you want your own space in the cottage a little longer." He looked genuinely distressed at the idea that I would leave the farm. "I know the right thing to do is let you go and then date you. And woo you." He gave me a lopsided grin. "You deserve that. But I can't imagine a day where I don't get to see you first thing in the morning and last thing at night. I can't imagine a time when we can't take a walk together and spend time with Benji together. I need you here. And I know you don't need it, but I want to give you this. A home. The freedom to do anything you want. If you don't want to cook or watch Benji, I can hire someone else. I want you to do whatever you want. I just want you to do it here. With me. Please say yes."

I was crying again. It was happening more and more. At some point I might become used to the loving things Max said to me, but that day hadn't come yet.

"Max," I said, getting out of my chair and settling myself onto his lap where he wrapped his arms around me. "I feel like everyone will think it's too soon, but ... yes. Yes, I'll stay with you." I slid my hand down his cheek and snaked it around to the back of his neck. "I'll stay with you and Benji on one condition."

"A condition?" he said. "What kind of condition?"

"That you stop paying me now for taking care of Benji." I sniffled a little and then kissed his cheek. "I adore spending time with him. I love him too, you know? I don't want a paycheck for that."

He looked thoughtful and then said, "Done. But I have a condition of my own."

I cocked my head to the side questioningly.

"You can't object when I buy you things. I've uprooted your entire life this summer. Again, I know you can take care of yourself, but I don't want you to. Okay? Can you let me a little?"

I touched his pink lips before kissing them. "Okay, lovely man. Okay."

We both jumped up when we heard Mr. Parker clear his throat. We turned to see Mr. and Mrs. Parker along with Benji standing at the threshold to the kitchen.

"I'm ready, Dad. Are we still gonna get ice cream when you pick me up tomorrow?"

"Yeah, buddy. Definitely. We'll go with Lanie, okay?"

"Yay!" Benji danced around the kitchen and started chattering about the games he and his grandparents were going to play that night and how they promised to take him for pizza for dinner.

Mrs. Parker stepped forward. "Lanie, could I have a quick word with you, please?"

"Mom," Max started, physically stepping between me and his mom. "I don't want—"

"Max, it's fine," I said. I stepped out from behind Max's imposing frame. "Should we take a little walk?"

***

"So that's it," Mrs. Parker – Pam, as she had insisted I start calling her – said. "I've let fear motivate me, and I've been horrible to you in the process. I'm really ashamed of myself. I've got no excuse except I love and want to protect my boys."

I couldn't believe the last ten minutes of my life. Pam had apologized and explained how fearful she was about Max getting into a bad situation. It didn't feel good that she thought I was the bad situation, but I could only feel affection toward her for wanting to protect Max and Benji.

"That sounds like a perfectly reasonable excuse to me," I said. "I really get it." I didn't believe Pam suddenly liked me, but I was willing to trust Max that this had been unusual behavior for his mom. And I could see the genuine anguish in her expression.

I was learning to value something about myself – I was resilient. Maybe my life had been filled with lots of things I wouldn't wish on anyone, but it had also taught me lots of things that I could see Max loved. I didn't hold grudges. I did have the ability to forgive and forget. I was relieved that Pam was extending the olive branch because it meant Max would feel so much weight lifted. I would do anything to make this better for him.

"When I first understood about Claudia," I said to her as we approached the house, "I was angry. Max told me how she hadn't been satisfied with her life here. And how she resented Benji. I still have a hard time with it. I've never met her, of course, and Max has told me lots of positive things about her. And she died! That's reason enough to just feel sorry about the situation. About her. But every time I think about her, I'm angry. I don't understand how someone could feel that way about Max and Benji. How anyone could not be grateful to be loved by Max."

"We'll have our own little club then," she said a little conspiratorially. "The club where we love and protect our boys. I should have trusted Max's judgment. Just because things went south with Claudia – it doesn't mean ... Max has always put others first. He's always paid attention to other people and their needs. Claudia took advantage of that. And I was afraid you were going to do that, too. I'm afraid of anyone doing that to him again. But I should have gotten to know you and not put that on you. I am sorry."

"I understand," I said. I felt like I was supposed to hug her or something. Solidify our truce and shared love for Max and Benji, but I just wasn't ready for that. I wasn't used to that. *Who are you to hug her*, my cruel little voice asked. I reached out to open the door to the house, but she stopped me.

She reached out and forced a hug on me. "We're going to be great friends, Lanie. Wait and see."

Chapter 18

"Sweetheart, I need to know more about your time with Ethan."

Max and I were finishing dessert at this Asian fusion restaurant he had taken me to. Their twist was using and showcasing local Maine ingredients – like fiddleheads when they were in season. Max had known half the farmers listed as suppliers on the back of the menu.

"I really don't want to make you think about it," he continued, "but I have to know how he hurt you. I need to make sure I'm careful. That I understand—"

"I get what you're saying," I replied, reaching over and caressing his hand to let him know it was okay.

"Ethan …" I started. "Ethan took advantage." I looked at Max and could see his face instantly harden. "Not like you're thinking, Max! If you're going to hear this, you have to stay calm. It's not as bad as you're thinking, and I can't tell you if it upsets you so much."

Max took several deep breaths and assured me he was calm. Even though his expression continued to betray him.

"Ethan took advantage of me, but he didn't force me. He didn't beat me. That's what you're thinking, I know. But it wasn't at that level. He was rough with me. Squeezed and pinched. Shoved and slapped a few times. But he didn't routinely hit me or anything like that. I think his dad did that to his mom, and I know now that's absolutely where it was headed. But that wasn't what it was like for us. He would get angry and use a little too much pressure or lose his temper and smack me. But it wasn't an everyday thing, and he didn't injure me or anything like that."

Max was fuming. His hands were squeezed into tight fists and his knuckles were bright white. His jaw was clenched so hard it had to hurt. "And the other? The *not* forcing?" he ground out.

"He manipulated me. If it was me now, today – yeah, it would be forcing. But … me then? I wanted to please him. I wanted to make him like me. Make him happy."

Max's eyes flashed black.

"He would put me down. Make me feel worthless. And when he initiated, he was persistent. It didn't matter how I was feeling, I would give in. I know that sounds terrible – for both of us. I'm trying to forgive myself for being so stupid. I was a kid. But really, Ethan was too. At least at first. And he had such a terrible example."

"Stop defending him," Max said in an anguished voice. "Please stop."

"That's it, Max. That's the whole story. I was vulnerable, and he saw an opportunity. And it's well behind me. Until recently, I hadn't seen him in four years."

"The time at Jessa's? That's the first time? And that's what started the spiral?"

"Yes. The spiral. So, I guess you're right – maybe it's not firmly behind me. But allowing him to make decisions for me. I was past that. That's what made him so angry. I had blocked him and avoided him all these years, and when we finally saw each other, I made it clear I wasn't an opportunity anymore."

We sat in silence for a few seconds. I watched Max absorb and process my past. He started to ask another question, but I cut him off. "Could we maybe talk about something else? I really don't like spending any energy on him. And I don't like making you upset. There's really nothing else to tell."

"What if it's sort of related? Is that okay?" Max asked.

"What do you mean?"

"Well, Lanie. Goddammit, every way I think to say this sounds wrong." He tapped his thumb against his dessert plate. "It's just – I don't want to push you if you have any ... *triggers* in that way. Jesus, you know how much I want you, but I can wait. You have to tell me what you want and when. I am a patient man. I'd wait as long as you needed. I just don't want to hurt you."

I was very clear in my mind how much I wanted Max and how much nothing he did triggered any past memories from my time with Ethan. And thinking about how much we both wanted each other made the burn of a blush creep from my neck all the way up my face.

"What I want ... When I want ..." I dropped my hands down to my lap and focused on them while Max's gaze bore into me. "Everything you do is perfect, Max. I want everything with you. There's nothing about being with you that's triggering. I want ... you." I raised my eyes to him without lifting my head. "Okay?"

"Check, please," he said softly and smiled at me.

"I ... I want to be an adult about this. I've never had an adult relationship – I know that's probably not something you want to hear, but it's true. I know we're supposed to talk about ... things."

"Things?" Max's eyebrows lifted.

"Things ... Things like I'm on the pill and I haven't been with anyone since ... since. Well, you know." I whispered this across the table, glancing around to make sure no one was near enough to hear what we were talking about.

Max's smile was wide now, and he had a gaze that was tender, reassuring. "I haven't been with anyone since Claudia."

"What?" I exclaimed louder than I intended. I had imagined a much more colorful past for him.

"What do you mean, 'What?'" he asked. "I have Benji, and I have the farm. And I haven't been looking for that. I wasn't looking for it when I found you. I had marked that part of my life off the list. At least until Benji was much older. But then you changed everything, Lanie."

The server brought over the check, and Max handed her his card immediately.

"And on that note," Max stood and put his hand out to me to help me up. "Let's go home."

***

"This little bed … I bought for you," Max said as he joined me on the bed in my little cottage. On the way home, I had asked if his bed was the same bed from when Claudia was alive. I was embarrassed to ask the question, but I really hated the idea of being with Max in his marital bed. We had been sleeping there the last few nights, and it had crossed my mind, but now with it being so intentional, it was hard to not ask. He had assured me it was not the same bed and then told me he liked that I had a bit of a jealous streak. I did. He then told me he was happy to spend our first night together in the cottage, though, and that we might as well recreate what should have been the last time we were there.

"You bought it for me?" I asked, snuggling into his warm, comforting body.

"I was losing my mind when I knew you were going to move in," he said stroking my arm. "The cottage was empty and dirty, and I was like a madman wanting to make it pretty for you. You're such a delicate, pretty little thing," he said, combing through my hair with his fingers. "And I needed it to be something you would like. I wanted you to feel comfortable."

I beamed up at him. "It worked. It was the loveliest thing I had ever seen. The loveliest place I've ever lived. And I've fought against calling it home since the day I showed up. Thank you, Max." I dropped kisses on his neck. "You didn't need to do any of that, but thank you so much."

We were wrapped up in each other under the yellow blanket he had chosen for my cottage. I felt another surge of appreciation for this man. Even when I thought he hated me, he had always been trying to take care of me. To make me feel good. I had shyly slipped off my dress before getting into the bed as quickly as I could in my bra and panties. He had done the same – stripped to his boxers before joining me. I was trying not to let my shyness overwhelm me. I wanted to be open with him. To enjoy every second we had together.

I reached up and took his face between my hands. "I love you, Max Parker. I'm so grateful I found you. And that you love me. And that you are patient with me."

"I love you, baby," he said as he rolled us over until he was covering me. "You can't know how many times, how many ways I've imagined this." He pressed himself against me and groaned. "All those times in the barn, after everyone cleared out. I wanted to push you up against the wall and just take from you. Every morning in the kitchen, I wanted to push you into the pantry and hide from Benji."

"That's a lot of pushing." I laughed as he kissed along my shoulders and shifted my bra strap down my arm.

"That first night I saw you in your little dress … I just wanted to drag it up inch by inch to peek at your little, sexy self." He was starting to get gruffer in his delivery, his voice losing its teasing lilt. "Fuck, Lanie, you're so goddamn sexy." He unclasped my bra and slid it away.

"The first time I saw you in the greenhouse. I could barely get through showing you how to do the work. I was so distracted by you. I hated myself. I kept telling myself you were off limits." He slid my panties down my legs and ran his fingers back up with a feather-light touch. "And that just made me want you more."

Everything was heightened. I could hear everything, smell everything, feel everything. My head felt all tingly and my body was on fire. "Max," I said. "Please. I need you." I started tugging at his boxers and he didn't waste time helping me get them off.

He was so close. We were so close. I looked up at him and kissed him. "I had no idea you felt that way. I thought you hated me for the longest time."

"No, baby. Myself. Hated myself for noticing such a sweet, young, innocent thing like you. I had no business pulling you into my life. You deserve uncomplicated and easy. But you've got me now – no turning back."

"You crazy man," I said, pulling him even closer to me. "You're all I could ever want. There's nothing complicated about you. You're simply good. That's it." We held each other's gaze long enough for me to see my eyes weren't the only ones that were glassy-eyed for a change.

"I love you so damn much, baby." He touched himself to me, and I wanted him with a burning I hadn't ever known.

"Are you ready, baby? Are you sure?"

"Yes, Max. Please now. I trust you. Please take care of me."

Max's expression turned fierce as he found his way to me. Finally.

"Jesus, fuck. That's so good. Baby, you feel so good."

I kissed Max and tried to adjust to him. He sensed what I needed and stilled, his face a mix of euphoria and pain. Time stood still while we both tried to wait out the sting, the shift, the transition from what was to what would be.

He began kissing me again, and I began to squirm underneath him, urging him to move again. I wanted him to possess me. I wanted to be connected to him forever, in every way possible. I just wanted to be his and wanted him to be mine.

"Sweet baby," Max muttered as he kissed and caressed and stroked. As we moved together, he gave me so much reassurance, so much tenderness. I was lost in a feeling of tingling and weightlessness and light, and I never wanted to leave it.

Finally, finally, the fire he had started deep within me spread and radiated outward, lighting up every part of me. I fought against my eyes that wanted to close so badly because as good as he was making me feel, watching him as he spilled into me felt even better. The face that I loved tensing and then growing softer and sweeter. It was a sight to behold, and it was now my favorite thing in the world.

Chapter 19

"You, sweetheart, have outdone yourself."

Max came up behind me and wrapped his arms around me. We looked out at the scene in front of us. The last few weeks on the farm had been the best kind of good. No one really seemed to care that Max was suddenly openly affectionate with me throughout the day. Apparently, they had expected it as much as Keisha had. Benji got his stitches out and ran around like the happy little boy that he was. We had been doing our usual things around the farm, but we had also spent time getting him ready to start kindergarten. Pam had asked if she could take him school shopping and if I would join them. I wouldn't say I felt comfortable and easy spending the day all together, but I was getting there. Pam really was the woman you would expect to be Max's mom. Now that she didn't see me as the enemy, she actually seemed to like me. She seemed to really care about me. And it had been fun working together to take care of Benji.

As we got closer to the end of August, I had an idea that I mentioned to Max, and it had grown from there. I had thought it would be nice to do something special for the students and crew beyond the last farm lunch we would share together. I mentioned a harvest dinner or something along those lines. All I had meant was that I would cook some special things, and we could make it a bigger meal at dinner, but Max took the idea to the next level.

What we ended up with was the joyful scene laid out in front of us. Farm tables and benches lovingly decorated by Benji and me and side tables groaning with food. I had made piles of pulled pork and a row of roast chickens. I hadn't wanted to dump all of Max's beautiful vegetables into chopped-up salads, so I roasted tray after tray of vegetables and focused on some special dipping sauces like lemon tahini and a bright dill tzatziki. There was every kind of potato – roasted, mashed, twice-baked – and loads of desserts. Several pies, piles of cookies, sheet pans of brownies and blondies, and triple-layer lemon blueberry cake.

This was all necessary because Max had invited far more people than the students and regular farmworkers. His parents had come, of course, but he also asked some friends of his, like his friend, Angela. She really was funny. He had also invited some other farmers and people from the Co-op, including Willow, whom I was happy to see again.

In addition to the dinner, Max had organized an area for some games for the kids, and Benji was thrilled to run around with them and show them every little thing. He also had an area that he had prepared with a small bonfire. There were stumps to use as stools and various benches and chairs in a big circle. Brendan was playing his guitar, and I was surprised but happy to see Keisha and Julian hanging out nearby in what looked like a very friendly conversation. The other students still made up their pack of four and were having a good time, despite the love triangle that seemed to persist. Rich had been making the rounds, looking for women to chat up. Max had been correct in his assessment there.

Looking at all of it and feeling Max's arms around me just made me happy. All the way happy. I couldn't believe I got to live this life.

"You're crazy, Max," I said to him. "I didn't do this. I just cooked some food like always. You created this … this event!"

"No, baby." Max nuzzled the back of my neck. "I can invite a bunch of people and throw some logs together to make a fire, but you did this. This has heart and beauty and magic. None of that was ever here before you."

I let his words wash over me. To know that I did that for him – it was everything.

"Look," he said, dropping his voice and practically whispering in my ear. "I want to marry you right now, but everyone will flip out, including you." He gripped me tighter as I jolted a bit in surprise.

"Wait, baby," he soothed. "Don't worry. I know it's too soon for you. So, I'll wait. I will. I won't even ask you yet. But you just need to know where this is headed. And, until then, you'll stay with us anyway. I don't care what anyone says. It's good for Benji for you to be in our lives and in our home. Everyone can see that anyway. I'll wait and give you what you need. I'll wait as long as it takes. I'm not afraid of losing you because I will simply not let you go. You can't go."

I slid my hands into Max's and hugged myself with our joined hands. He knew me. He had known me a few short months, but already knew me better than anyone had in my entire life. The idea of marrying this man, of being in Benji's life forever – I was so grateful.

"Lanie, hey," Willow said as she approached us. "Max, this is great. Thanks for inviting our crew. I think everyone is having a great time."

Max and I both greeted Willow, and I felt Max give my arm an extra squeeze. I knew he was remembering that I thought they would make a good couple. He still teased me sometimes, and I was learning to appreciate it – to know it was one way he showed his love for me. But he also knew

when I needed reassurance, and this was him letting me
know he wasn't laughing at me.

"Lanie, the food is so good. I knew you were keeping
everyone happy over here – I keep hearing about it every
time someone comes into the shop. Keisha showed me your
Instagram page, too. Such great shots. You do an amazing
job playing up local ingredients."

"Thanks, Willow," I said. "That's so nice of you to
say."

"Well, it's not just me being nice. I actually kind of
have a business proposition for you."

I looked at Willow, stunned. A business proposition?
Was there an opening at the Co-op? I mean, that would be
better than the coffee shop. And close to Max's where,
apparently, I was staying so …

"So, you know we sell locally made, prepared food,
right?" she continued. "I was thinking you might want to sell
some things at the Co-op. The licensing is really easy. You
can only do shelf-stable stuff if you make it in a home
kitchen, but if there's a place somewhere around here you
could designate as a separate kitchen, you could do anything
you wanted." Willow looked around at all the outbuildings
around the farm while she spoke, including my little cottage.

"Wow," I began. "Wow, that's really …" Amazing! Life-changing! My dream job? How did I respond to something that I wanted so badly? "Would that be okay, Max?" I shifted in his arms so I could see his face. "For me to cook things here to sell at the Co-op? Things will slow down since the students are leaving and it would be good … I could do it while Benji's at school. Maybe?"

Max smiled at me and said, "Anything you want, sweetheart. We could put a full kitchen in the cottage."

Willow asked for my phone number and said she'd send me links to some information about getting started, and I wanted to hug her before she let us know she had to take off. I was still me, so I didn't actually reach out and hug her, but I tried to tell her as much as I could with my words and big smile.

Max turned me all the way toward him after Willow left, so we were looking straight at each other.

"Baby," he said. "I want you to feel comfortable asking me – no, telling me – whatever it is you want. How you want to spend your time. What you want to do in the future. You can do this thing for Willow, or go to college if you want, or do abso-fuckin-lutely nothing. You deserve to do anything you want, and I want to make that happen for you. It would be my honor – yes, my goddamn honor," he grinned, and I knew we were both remembering our earlier conversation about Jessa's family. "My honor to do that for you. But one thing I know – I don't want you going back to the coffee shop. You don't like it there. You never say anything, but you dread going and come home tired. And I miss you when you're there. Will you consider it?"

I couldn't be happier doing anything other than what I had been doing this summer. Knowing it actually helped Max and made him happy was what I needed to be able to tell him that.

"I want … I guess I want to keep doing what I'm doing," I said, looking up at him. "I love being here. I love taking care of Benji – and you, if you'll let me. And I love cooking, so if I could do that instead of the coffee shop, that would make me really happy."

"Yeah?" Max asked, bending down to kiss me. "I think I need you to take care of me as soon as I can get this crowd out of here."

"Max!" I squealed as he twirled me around a bit.

Milo jumped up against us and barked, thinking we were playing. Benji came running up right behind him.

"Lady Lanie," Benji excitedly greeted me. "My friend showed me some new tricks we can teach Milo. Can we work on them tomorrow? Dad, you too? Can we play with Milo tomorrow?"

Max nodded, and I said, "Yes, sweet Benji. I can't wait."

Epilogue

Max

I pulled the ring box from its hiding place and looked at it for the millionth time. I had bought it months ago – right after I convinced Lanie to stay. I wanted to marry her then and there, but I knew it was too soon for her. The ring sparkled in its little box – a white gold band with a solitaire diamond. Simple but stunning. Just like my girl.

It was Christmas Eve, and I couldn't wait any longer. Even though I told her I could be patient. The proposal was happening tonight. I would have asked her in front of everyone at Christmas Eve dinner with my parents, or I would have taken her to a restaurant or somewhere special to ask her because I would love to make a big deal out of her. To celebrate her. But I knew she would hate it. She bloomed under my attention but still closed up and felt nervous if there were too many eyes on her. It would have to wait until after the dinner. After Benji went to bed.

"Daddy, what's that?" Benji came into my room, and I immediately shushed him, nervously looking to see if Lanie had come upstairs with him. Seeing it was all clear, I sat on the end of the bed and motioned for Benji to jump up and join me.

"It's a ring, bud. For Lanie. But you need to keep it a secret until tomorrow, okay?"

"For marrying? That kind of ring?"

"Yeah, buddy. I'm gonna ask Lanie to marry me tonight. Do you think she'll say yes?"

"Lanie always says yes when you ask her something, so I think probably yes."

I laughed at the less-than-flattering truth my son spoke. It was true. Lanie was still very agreeable. But I was always thrilled to see when she put her foot down on something or when she gave me a little grief. It was rare, but it was happening more often. She was feeling more comfortable and more sure of her place every day.

"What do you think about us getting married? Would you like that?"

"Would Lanie be my mom?"

"I think if you ask her. She always says yes when you ask her something," I bandied right back to my boy.

"I love her, Daddy. I want her to be my mom and to stay with us always. But you have to ask her nice. She sometimes says no now. Sometimes."

After Benji headed back downstairs, promising to keep the secret, I put the ring away again and felt my throat tighten. I felt the prick of tears threatening to break free. I was so damn grateful for her. I had never in my life been so happy.

When I first saw her, it was like a battle between being angry that the universe would set something so amazing in front of me that I couldn't have and just being happy that I got to see her. The way she forced past her shyness to stick up for her friend. Her worthless friend. The way she worried about Benji before she even knew him. And then she was just so pretty on top of all of that.

I knew I didn't deserve her. I was a decent guy. I tried to keep my temper. Be a good dad. Be good to the people who worked for me. But I had thoughts. Fuck, I still had thoughts about that Ethan clown. The things I wanted to do to him …

My Lanie, though – she still tried to defend him. And his sister. That whole damn family. She was always reminding me of the obstacles they'd had in their lives. How they had taken her in when she needed a place to stay. And damnit, she meant it. That's truly what she was made of. That kind of love, forgiveness, goodness.

"Max," she said, stepping into our room. She was wearing a snowy white dress with a belt around her waist. She looked like a beautiful little elf, and I felt like a bad Santa. "Are you ready to go? I have all the food ready to take to your parents' house. We just need to load up the truck."

I couldn't wait. There was no way I could sit through dinner and wait to do this.

"Lanie, come here, baby." I pulled her farther into the room.

"Max, what is it?" She looked closely at me and then put her delicate hand to my forehead. "Are you okay? You look a little pale."

I let out a laugh. "I'm fine, sweetheart. At least I hope I'll be fine in just a minute. Come here. Stand right here." I pulled her to the center of the room and turned my back to her to take out the ring again.

"Max, what's going on? Benji's going to swipe the frosting right off the cake if we don't get downstairs and—"

I turned toward her and went down on a knee. I was in such a damn hurry. I tried to slow myself down. To calm myself down.

I looked up at Lanie and her eyes were huge. Her face always showed everything she felt. She once asked me how I knew how to give her what she needed. You just had to pay attention. It was all written right there if you just looked.

"Lanie, you look surprised, but I don't know how you can be. I have wanted to do this for a long time, and I've told you that. I couldn't keep that to myself. Baby, I've waited as long as I can. I don't want to rush you, but I need to ask you."

She was swaying a little, wobbly on her feet. And I doubt she knew it, but she was robotically nodding her head up and down.

"Lanie Billings. Will you please wear this ring and marry me very soon? I know lots of men have said this before me, but you would truly be making me the happiest man on earth."

Lanie's slow nodding hadn't stopped, but she didn't say anything for a bit. I took her left hand and pulled it toward me. I didn't want to rush her, but I was willing to nudge. I pulled the ring from the box and started to slip it on her finger.

As I slid it slowly on, she kept up the nodding, and tears joined in. They streaked down her cheeks. I got the ring fully on and asked, "Is that a yes, Lanie?"

"Yes," she whispered. "Yes, I will."

I stood to take her into my arms, but suddenly Benji was there hugging our legs with Milo wagging his tail behind him. "Does this mean I can call you Mom now?" Benji asked.

Lanie picked him up and brought him into our hug.

"Yes, my little boy. If you'd like to. Absolutely. You and your daddy are my family now. I'm finally home, and I'm here to stay."

Dear Reader,

I hope you enjoyed *Reluctant Bloom*! A second Farm to Table book is in the works. Please leave me a note in the reviews and subscribe to my email list for updates about upcoming books and more!

https://www.arabellspencer.com/newsletter

You can find me on Facebook and Instagram. You might even see some of Lanie's creations there! Thanks to AD and thank *you* for reading.

Arabell

Printed in Great Britain
by Amazon

24089943R00172